THE POSSE
A Story of Love — and Resistance

by Todd Parnell

Acclaim Press
MORLEY, MISSOURI

Acclaim Press
— *Your Next Great Book* —

P.O. Box 238
Morley, MO 63767
(573) 472-9800
www.acclaimpress.com

Editor: Charlie Francis
Cover art: "Politics" by Betty Parnell
Book Design: Rodney Atchley

Library of Congress Control Number: 2020946676
ISBN: 978-1-948901-74-1 / 1-948901-74-9

First Printing 2020
Printed in the United States of America
10 9 8 7 6 5 4 3 2 1

This publication was produced using available information.
The publisher regrets it cannot assume responsibility for errors or omissions.

CONTENTS

DEDICATION

Dedicated to Four Egrets and a Blue Heron

As my daughter and her friend recently slipped and slid down late summer Swan Creek in southwest Missouri, falling occasionally, on an ill-advised attempt to kayak the beautiful bedrock bottomed crystal waters, they were joined by first one, then two, three, and finally four white egrets and a blue heron, a natural support squad of sorts circling above, to bring them safely home to Casey hole. I have occasionally felt a similar circle of support along the way to the end of this story.

Todd Parnell, Summer, 2020

Chapter One

SHOTS

A shot rang out. A pig squealed. Another shot. Another pig squeal. Ten more of each in a row, just before dawn.

"Sheriff Silas, it's the same damn thing. Someone shot a dozen more of my hogs through the curtained windows of my containment house last night. Just like last month. I don't get it. With 6,500 head it barely makes a ripple in this round of profits, but it seems so intentional. Almost like someone is sending a message."

"Have you thought about posting a guard, Jimmy?"

"For twelve pigs? They wouldn't even cover the cost. No, I want you to do something, Sheriff. You're the law enforcement around here. Enforce it. It's surely not legal to go around shooting a man's hogs, is it? Am I the only one?"

"Funny you should ask, Jimmy. No, you're not. It started about six months ago. Random targets and time intervals. Always at night. First it was a CAFO owner down in Northwest Arkansas, hogs like yours. Then another just west of here. Same thing every time. Shoot a dozen singletons in the middle of the night and beat it. I've had a dozen reports in addition to yours, and my counterparts throughout the Ozarks acknowledge the same. It is like you said—almost messaging. I just wish they would speak plain English, so I could understand. Whatever the case, I want you to keep this quiet, Jimmy. No sense in spooking our sponsors or you guys on the ground. Too much at stake. Trust me. I'll get to the bottom of it all."

Chapter Two

COMING HOME

The squinty eyes stared back at her from the face of a large lit-up pig on a neon billboard sign. The caption beneath read "PORK CAPITAL OF THE WORLD." This just as Penelope Plum pulled off the Interstate onto Exit 75, which would take her back to her family's old hometown. She had known that this is what would await her return to live after thirty years on the East Coast, but it still shocked her.

Penny, as she went by, simply couldn't stand Boston anymore. She had kicked around there for several years after completing her education, both teaching and writing, but it was time to move on. She loved her mom and dad, but both were deeply ensconced in the entertainment world, loving life and each other too much to leave any of it.

As an only child, Penny had been raised in a middle-class neighborhood just south of town on the way to the Cape, which was the one landscape she would miss. She had loved walking the lonely beaches there after the tourists had left for the season and, in fact, had lost her virginity on one to a high school sweetheart her senior year. Though they had moved on from each other, the memory was sweet, if a bit sandy.

Penny had been educated in the area from pre-K through an advanced degree in history from Clark University. Clark had been perfect for her. A small liberal arts university with innovative flexibility of curriculum had allowed her to pursue her keen interest in family roots back in the Missouri and Arkansas Ozarks in the context of her path to knowledge. Ten generations worth.

She had excelled at Clark and particularly impressed her professors with an ability to link and incorporate her passion for family history into other courses of study along the way.

By the time she had completed her master's in history, Clark science faculty were intimately familiar with Skunk Creek, Weasel Creek, Swine Branch, Large Creek, Cottonmouth Creek, and the like. They understood the cleansing power of the Ozarks karst topography, as well as the vulnerability to degradation of surface and ground water that was its by-product. And they had grieved with her at the fouling of pristine waters that had accompanied a large expansion of corporate agriculture in the region.

Geography professors were introduced to tiny villages like Hardlyville, Niche, and Welcome and their colorful populations of Hardlyvillians, Nichees, and Welcomers. They learned of the debate about where the Ozarks extended to and from and the endless theories in support of including or excluding Northeast Oklahoma or Southeast Missouri. And they learned that America's first and only "National River" was situated in Northwest Arkansas. That the Buffalo National River had survived despite government efforts to dam her in the 1960s and corporate agriculture's efforts to pollute her in the early 2000s. Penny's roots ran particularly deep in that watershed, way back into the 1830s.

At her suggestion, English and literature instructors began to introduce authors like Vance Randolph, Donald Harrington, Daniel Woodrell, Brooks Blevins, and Randi Philander into mainstream courses to add color and depth to curriculum.

With Penny's research and encouragement, business professors began to present the Ozarks as a case study of what could go wrong in a relatively pristine natural environment with the virtual elimination of regulation and oversight at both state and local levels. They could track the concentration of the pork industry into the hands of several large international conglomerates, from Brazil to China to mainline USA, and their export of more than half of all pork production to China. They could document the vertical and horizontal integration of the meat industry, the expansion of factory farms into new and previously undeveloped markets and supply chains, and the concentration of wealth that accompanied this unfettered growth. They could demonstrate the environmental and societal costs of this transition from traditional farming to an oligarchy business model that curtailed competition and bred concentration.

Sadly and ironically, mid-sized Spring Town, Missouri, served as the perfect case in point. For now a few billionaire scions of meat processing and exporting fame had overrun the historical stable of successful entrepreneurs, born of a water-based economy tied to the tourism, recreation, and supporting service industries of her earlier days. Research confirmed that the decline in overall property values related to CAFO (confined animal feeding operation) expansions and led to reduced tax revenues and a resultant deterioration in the provision of public services. And that poverty had spread throughout the region as measured by high unemployment, free and reduced lunch rates of greater that 70% in Spring Town and neighboring school districts, and an overall poverty rate of nearly 30%. Professors could posit that the economic development model that concentrated wealth and spread such misery rewarded short-term thinking and long-term degradation of critical natural resources. Especially water. Fresh, clean, healthy water and the tourist and recreation industry that it had spawned long ago. Spring Town had become but a shadow of its former prosperous and healthy self.

Political science instructors could create a real-time look at the power and money of lobbyists, bought and sold state legislators, agricultural trade associations and bureaus, as well as their efforts to deregulate and incentivize chosen business segments, like corporate agriculture, in order to foster select concentrations of financial power.

Health and Wellness faculty took interest in, and shared in classes, Penny's detailed documentation of the warning signs of deteriorating health markers, from juvenile asthma to chronic dysentery, and related deterioration of air and drinking water quality. Nitrate contamination in groundwater, the by-product of disposal of millions of tons of animal waste on application fields, was blamed for increases in miscarriages, birth defects, and certain cancers.

There was even evidence of pockets of local residents' resistance to antibiotics that entered the biosphere through waste polluted water.

And through it all, Penny Plum became the catalyst for focus on a little-known corner of the world, at least to Eastern intellectuals, and how bad things could become so very quickly.

It was her master's thesis that pulled it all together. She provided a comprehensive treatise on economic development gone wrong in the Ozarks in the context of national and international trends. The Missouri and Arkansas Ozarks had traded in a multimillion-dollar economy keyed to water-based tourism and recreation and conductive to traditional family farming for a similarly sized economy grounded in huge concentrations of pigs and chickens, with the resultant degradation in quality of life, from a health, property value, and lifestyle perspective. Penny documented the tragic transition in graphic detail. It was soon published and enthusiastically received in an environmentally niched literary market. Naturally, she had earned an A.

The year was 2030, and Penny Plum was moving back "home." Home in the sense of roots and history. Why? She wasn't sure given all the unfortunate changes that had occurred.

She had spent parts of many of her growing up summers with relatives—at first g. randparents, and after they were gone, aunts, uncles, and cousins. It had provided an idyllic counterbalance to the teeming Northeast. She had learned to fish for smallmouth bass; to hunt squirrels and rabbits; to fillet, skin and fry them all. She had become proficient with canoe and kayak and loved setting up a tent on a gravel bar and cooking on an open fire.

The longest float trip she took in her teens was four days and three nights with her grandparents on the lower Buffalo River. Just the three of them. It had been a magical ride, she in her kayak, they in canoe with gear. They were slowing down but managed to keep everything high and dry. She did most of the setup and takedown. They watched with pride and encouraged her independence as they always had. She grieved greatly when they passed, one shortly after the other. Together again, as through all those years.

And again when her aunts and uncles moved away with their children, nauseated at what their homeland had become. One uncle had migrated to Idaho to regain access to some semblance of natural beauty and order. Another uncle chose an urban area in the Midwest. One with all the amenities of the big city and enough parks to provide their children with fresh air. And more murders per capita than any metropolitan area in the country.

Penny's homecoming high was tempered by the reality of what she was returning to. She moved in temporarily with an old friend from childhood who had lived through the whole devastation and still clung to past. She was an elementary school teacher who had witnessed up close and personal the impact on a generation of youngsters, year by year, decade by decade. The loss of hope and eventual abandonment of roots had scarred her deeply.

Spring Town billionaires, sickness and poverty, a soured water table. It all blew her mind as she recalled happier times gone by.

One early fall afternoon she visited her grandparents' gravestones in a small cemetery tucked atop a bluff fronting a stagnated creek. She parked at the base of the dirt road that led to them and slowly climbed up. At least this was a peaceful and safe space, untouched by time, with markers dating back to the 1850s.

She then walked down to the creek. The one she used to frolic and splash in, before graduating to a canoe with her grandfather and then her uncles and then proudly in the stern by herself. The old swimming hole, named in honor of her earliest ancestors to homestead the area, was still there. But the creek showed chunks of thick green algae globed along the far bank. A faint odor of decay floated above the surface. She winced.

It was just like my grandfather had predicted it would be, Penny thought to herself. "It's our lifeblood at risk," he had ranted to anyone who would listen back in the days when things were coming apart. "Water is, has, and will always be the lifeblood of the Ozarks." Obviously too few had paid attention. Or cared.

Penny begin to sob, tears leaking. Lost in memories of places and loved ones long past.

A strong hand on her left shoulder brought her back to here and now.

"What's a pretty lady like you doing crying?"

"Who are you?"

"Sammy. Sammy Spode. Again, what's made you so sad?"

"Memories. I learned to swim in this putrid hole of water when I visited my grandparents and my aunts and uncles, long ago. Look at it now."

"I grew up swimming here as well. My best friend Lenny Cagy claimed to have ancestral rights to this stretch of creek, going back to the 1800s. Said his family was among the original settlers buried just up the hill there. I thought he was making it up but humored his attempts to grow roots."

"He wasn't making it up, Sammy Spode. He must have been a relative of mine, a little older as I recall. I don't remember him well. My grandparents and those before them are buried in that same small family cemetery up that dirt road. It was all true what Lenny Cagy told you."

"So, who are you, pretty lady? What's your name? And why were you standing here crying moments ago? Do you live here? Are you just visiting for old times' sake?"

"You ask lots of questions, stranger. My name is Penny Plum, and I just moved back into town several weeks ago. And, yes, I had to see for myself what others had told me about this precious piece of my childhood. Who did this? Who ruined Goose Creek? Who allowed them to do it? Is it like this everywhere?"

"Now you're the one firing questions. And it will take more than one response to begin to answer them. Can I buy you a beer?"

Chapter Three
A FRIEND

Penny Plum took an immediate liking to Sammy Spode. He was handsome, in a down-home-country kind of way, though that was not the seed of her attraction. His torn baggy jeans and spotted T-shirts adorned a tall, slender frame that seemed to slide rather than stride through space.

It was his curiosity and subtle sense of humor that engaged her interest and provoked her openness to him.

Penny had blown through enough young men in her life that she was wary of any intention, expressed or not. Simply asking her to share a beer had set the caution flags to waving behind Sammy's engaging smile. As his interest in finding out more about her carried on beyond their initial encounter and took on the feel of genuine, she began to drop her guard. And enjoy doing so. A male she could trust. Not just yet she told herself. He is a man after all.

Her last one, a Yankee blue blood named Peter Whisnut, III had in the end been just that. A nut—and a selfish, brutish one at that. It had taken Penny two years and an engagement with plans to be married at his country estate in upstate New York to figure out that their lack of shared values did not bode well for a lasting relationship.

They had met at Clark and reconnected through old friends a few years later in whirlwind fashion. A couple of trips to exotic locales set Penny's head to spinning. Peter was charming and fawning one moment, then slipping off to bed with one of those old friends the next, as Penny later discovered. That it had taken Penny so long to see through Peter Whisnut III's thin veneer had shaken her self-confidence and, in the end, had helped send her running westward to the home she had only known through others. And yet a home that she was deeply rooted in over ten generations. And to Sammy Spode amongst other things.

From Sammy's perspective, his new acquaintance was a friend not a conquest. He was different that way. Not that he hadn't had his share of lovers or even prospective life partners. He just didn't equate the two and preferred friendship to pleasure or security. Penny seemed to fit into that context, at least for now. He liked her and enjoyed her company.

—ɯ—

"So, Sammy, what do you really like to do? More than anything?" Penny had asked during their third or fourth evening of shared suds and conversation.

"You really want to know?"

"Yes. What would you do tomorrow if you didn't have a job or any obligations?

"Go floatin'. Load up my old metal Grumman canoe with a tent, bedroll, cooler of cold beverage, and enough food for five or six days in case I didn't catch any fish and shove off. No schedules or deadlines—just me and the river and my truck waiting for me when I decide to come in. Now of course I would be hoping for fair days and maybe a little rain during the night to keep the creek flush and flowing but not much more. Oh, yes, I'd take my deer rifle along to pop any nasty cottonmouths that showed their heads."

Penny smiled. "You know I learned to paddle a canoe, hold a fishing pole, and a cold beer all at once by the time I was sixteen. My uncles taught me during summers with my grandparents. It's one thing I missed living out East. The rivers are too big, the creeks too small, and those who like to camp and paddle prefer lakes. I missed it a lot."

"Wanna go sometime, Ms. Penny? Doesn't need to be for days at a time. I promise not to tip you … or come on to you."

"Most men I've known are liars," Penny responded with a slight smile.

Chapter Four

A FLOAT TRIP

Penny drove her car, with Sammy's canoe rack atop, to the last halfway bearable downstream take-out spot left on Goose Creek. Her old family swimming hole. So much personal stuff at play here. She was pleased that Sammy had chosen this stretch to float. She had done so long before, albeit a shorter iteration. There were no other cars or trucks in sight, which spoke to a solitary journey to come. She locked up and walked back to Sammy's truck, with his canoe hanging out the back. He nodded with a smile and added, "Looks like we'll have her all to ourselves."

The "sometime" he had suggested had come quickly. Penny had no job to seek permission to skip, and Sammy was a self-employed general repairman. He could fix about anything that was broken, he had claimed, without a trace of braggadocio and was between engagements, which afforded him as much time off as he wanted. It had taken them several days to gather equipment and supplies. Penny had to buy the basics but thought it was a good investment for future activity. A sleeping bag, duffle, and—in the interest of propriety—her own tent. They had to plan around a weather front that dumped a couple of inches of rain and muddied things up a bit, but the trailing cooldown would be good for the fishing Sammy had promised. It would help keep the beer cooler ice from melting so fast as well. "Can't have enough cold beer," Sammy promised.

They would plan on about twenty river miles from put-in to take-out, likely four days and three nights, with enough food to stay longer if needed. Going midweek would keep the river traffic down as well.

"I'm really excited to get back on the river after all of these years, Sammy. Thanks for taking me!"

"You are pretty brave to take it on. I don't know many young ladies who would slip away into nature for the better part of a week with a near stranger. You hardly know me, you realize. I could be a psychopath or manic depressive, schmoozing you one minute and drowning you the next."

"I'll take my chances on that, Sammy Spode. Just don't stare when I take my daily river bath."

"What? You do that too? I mean, strip naked and soap up in the creek every day?"

"I wasn't raised to be sweaty and smelly at home, at work, or on the river."

"You was sure raised right then!"

First day out was glorious, water clear and fast, sun warming not baking. Fishing could have been better but lagged because of the recent weather change. Still Penny managed to land a six-teen-inch smallmouth bass late in the afternoon, which set her to giggling with glee. Sammy had paddled her around most of the day, showing her where to toss her twin tailed grub, and only occasionally flipping his topwater minnow imitation along the edges of swift water. They rarely spoke and were passed by only two other canoes, who seemed in a hurry. The peace and solitude embraced them both.

Setting up camp was a precursor to division of duties to come. A campfire was the first priority.

Penny gathered wood. Sammy dug the fire pit and lit the match. Each raised their tents on opposite sides of the fire to afford some privacy. Sammy threw chunked potatoes and carrots wrapped in foil into the fire once it settled. Penny tossed a salad in a bag. Both sat down in camping chairs and had a cold beer. Sammy then proceeded to grill two bone-in strip steaks rare. They ate in silence around the fire, chewing directly from the bone and occasionally glancing skyward to the star-spangled sky. Juices dripped from their chins, glistening in the dancing firelight.

"So, how did this upper part of the stream remain so clean and pristine with what's gone on around it?"

"Well, most of it is surrounded on both sides by the Mark Twain National Forest, and even corporate ag hasn't been able to penetrate that shield of protection. It's not for lack of trying. The one-term crazy-ass president we had a while back pushed an agenda to take back public lands from the people and open them to all sorts of intrusions from mining, drilling, fracking, logging, grazing, and large-scale farming. He was somewhat successful in red rock southwest country, raiding and degrading national parks and monuments, including even the Grand Canyon. Thankfully he was thrown out after one term of a national nightmare, and sanity was restored as relates to our country's precious environmental treasures. And he never did make it as far as the Ozarks and our large national forest cover, again thankfully. You know, your ancestors chose well settling on this special creek centuries back. As you know, we take out at that hole of water below where they are buried on our last day. The very place I first met you, as you cried your pretty eyes out. You've seen how the water quality deteriorates downstream where the protective national forest buffer ends."

"I'm getting sleepy, Sammy. Think I will head off to my sleeping bag."

"Rest well, Penny. I'm going to have one more nightcap beer."

Next morning dawned bright and bracing. Penny and Sammy feasted on cereal and fruit, chased with the darkest, richest coffee Penny had ever tasted. Sammy had dipped his old blue coffee pot in the creek, brought the water to a boil, pulled it off the fire, dropped two handfuls of grind in it, let it sit for exactly ten minutes, and with a flair of showmanship, sprinkled cold water in to sink grounds to the bottom. Penny loved it.

As Sammy sat sipping cup number three and contemplating taking tents down and packing up, Penny emerged from hers wrapped only in a towel, which she dropped before wading in and submerging. Sammy was struck frozen in the moment. He simply had never seen a more beautiful sight in all his time on the river. Not the twenty-inch smallmouth he had caught several years back. Not the sunsets, the rises, the blanket of stars sandwiched between, not the white spray of a raging rapid.

He tried to shut his eyes, but they wouldn't close. He turned his head to the side only to feel it snap back reflexively into place. Penny waved to him. He blushed and waved back before burying his face in his coffee cup.

Penny emerged from the water and quickly rewrapped the towel around her, stepping gingerly on gravel between her and the tent. She flashed a smile and said cheerfully, "You promised not to gawk."

It was all Sammy could do to move toward his own tent for dismantling without glancing over his shoulder.

Nothing more was said as camp was collapsed and loaded into the canoe, fire extinguished, and campsite scoured clean.

Day two passed with all the beauty and a few more fish than the first. As sun sunk, Sammy picked up the pace of his paddling, from piddle to stroke. He had a favorite gravel bar to camp on that night. He doubted that anyone had beaten him to it, because they had seen just two canoes all day. -It was empty and as stunning as he had promised Penny. Racing rapid spreading into a broad, deep pool, facing bluff reflecting setting sun, all directly across from where Sammy dug a firepit. Penny gathered firewood. Sammy lit the match. Both erected tents on opposite sides of the campfire as they had the evening before. Both sat down in fold-up chairs and sipped a beer. But this night Penny retreated to her tent, half-finished beer in hand, emerged with towel slung over her bare shoulder, and lowered her naked body into the clear pool of water. She motioned for Sammy to join her. He sat dumbstruck for a moment, then scrambled to his feet, dropped his shorts and shirt on the ground, and moved slowly toward the water.

"You are the most beautiful thing I have ever seen," he mumbled to Penny.

She smiled and waved him forward again.

"So, if we do this, Penny, if we go through with this, will you still be my friend?"

"More than ever, Sammy, more than ever."

Several things rolled around in Sammy's mind in the afterglow of the evening, Penny tucked in next to his chest. They certainly wouldn't need to bring two tents on their next float trip. And he was glad they had packed an extra day of food. He simply didn't want this trip to ever end.

Chapter Five

A RELATIONSHIP

"So, where did you go when you slipped out of bed at 2 a.m. last night?"

"I don't think you want to know, Penny."

"Another woman?"

—⚇—

It didn't take Penny and Sammy long to comingle and cohabit their lives.

Sammy had fallen heart over crotch in love with Penny on Goose Creek. He wanted her next to him every night when he tucked in and every morning when he first stirred. His feelings for Penny were unlike any he had ever experienced with another woman. He wore them in his eyes and his smile, and expressed them in his insatiable lust.

Penny, on the other hand, was a bit more cautious with giving all of herself away. She had been burned enough before, and the most recent flameout, which had sent her scrambling for the Ozarks, had left scars. She really liked Sammy. She shared his love of the outdoors and all that went with that. She liked his cooking, which began to spoil her. And she adored his childish shy side, which featured a bizarre sense of humor and self. And the way he looked at her, the way he held her, the way he loved her weren't hard to take either. She was just wary of pedestals and the threat of falling that was always present. In the end, she loved their time together and supposed that was a sort of love in itself.

Having moved in with Sammy after a short spell of frequent visitations, Penny felt the need to earn some income to help with the rent, the food and drink, and shared life in general.

So, she took a job as a beat writer for the flailing *Spring Town Gazette*, her beat being anything that the editor wanted her to cover at any time of day or night, as well as a weekly column on ... anything the editor wanted her to write about. She enjoyed the writing part if not the odd hours away from Sammy, but his freelance work schedule accommodated most of her assignments. They settled into a routine that was never very routine but did little to douse their growing shared passion.

Sammy's circle of hometown friends, including a couple of ex-girlfriends, embraced Penny as one of their own. They were an odd lot, some educated, some not, which left her feeling like an elitist outlier on occasion, but there didn't seem to be a mean or jealous bone amongst the lot. After a couple of months, Penny confessed to herself that she had never been happier in her life.

She was probably in love, grounded in the history of her homeland, encircled with kindness and affection, and getting to write for a living.

But then there was the spoiled water, the fouled air, the wafting odor of waste that seemed to periodically settle over her new life.

—⁓—

"They did it again last night, Sheriff Silas, just before dawn I reckon, as everything was okay when I checked in at 2 a.m., as I've taken to doing. Just like before. An even dozen hogs. Shot dead as shit. What are you going to do about it, Sheriff? This has been going on for too many months."

"I know."

Chapter Six

A POSSE

"So, where did you go at 2 a.m. last night, Sammy Spode? Don't deny it because I heard you get up and sneak out. You barely made it back before dawn. I need to know if there is another woman involved, no matter how much it might hurt."

"It's not another woman, Penny. There could be no other woman. You are it for me."

"So, where in the hell were you, Sammy?"

"It's a long and self-incriminating story that I prefer to spare you of. It may have consequences eventually. You don't deserve any of them."

"How about you allow me to decide that?"

"I just don't know, Penny. I have sworn not to."

"How about I swear not to tell anyone? Does that help?"

"I'm not sure. If I swear not to and do, why wouldn't you do the same?"

Sammy squeezed his hands on his head and walked away. Penny sat tight and said nothing. She heard the toilet flush and footsteps returning.

"You're going in circles, Sammy. Either you trust me or you don't. And if you don't, we have larger problems than keeping secrets."

"OK, Penny. I was out shooting pigs."

"Say what?" Penny responded in disbelief.

"I was out shooting pigs, exactly like I said. An even dozen of them. In a CAFO not far from here, one that has been personally assigned to me. It is owned and managed by Jimmy Johnson, a local businessman, who agreed to front for a large Brazilian pork-producing conglomerate a while back, and now employs a few hired hands, mostly Mexicans, to feed and raise 6,500 pigs at a time for the Brazilians to process and sell to China. Mr. Jimmy is one of the new landed gentry in the Ozarks, having bought up small farms and acreages with foreign-sourced cash over the past decade. I knew him when he had a simple construction company and occasionally subbed jobs for him. I was friends with one of his sons, who has since moved on. So, there is a personal connection for me to take out my personal animosity on."

"You are just doing this on your own, Sammy?"

"No, there is an informal network of thirty or forty of us around the Ozarks who are taking on the bosses, the ones who have ruined our homeland. We maintain anonymity, collectively and amongst each other. I don't know a single other 'assassin' for lack of a better word. I have some suspicions but not certainty. I just know that when the word gets texted out at irregular intervals, we are sworn to taking out an even dozen of our assigned 'sugar daddy's' herd or flock at an appointed time in the middle of the night. The Posse we call ourselves, a statement of our renegade status and our passion for justice.

"So, why don't I ever hear anything about this in my reporter role? Surely this is newsworthy. I have never even caught a whiff of any of this."

"The head of the local pig bureau chapter, Deacon Duncan, who is also pastor of the True Church of Christ, owns the newspaper with a couple of his ag-friendly buddies. For some reason they have determined that if word got out about a counter-CAFO underground culture in the Ozarks, it would scare off potential investors. So, they live in a world of denial, hoping we will just go away. The local sheriff, a bumbling idiot name of Sheriff Silas Slack, and several of his counterparts around the area have tried to set traps for us—you know, lure us in for easy kills and capture, but our collective discipline has not failed yet. We follow our orders quickly and efficiently and disappear into bed. In my case with the most beautiful woman in the world."

"Who gives those orders, Sammy? Who is the mastermind behind this cruelty-to-animals scheme?"

"You know, I don't know. And don't really want to. I just want to send a message that it is not okay what they have done in the name of money to our water, to our air, to our health, to our property values. That their self-serving ways do not go unnoticed."

"Do you enjoy shooting pigs, Sammy?"

"Not really. I kind of feel sorry for them and their little squeals. And I would much rather be plunking Jimmy Johnson in his fat ass. But that could get me in some real trouble."

Penny reached out to Sammy and pulled him down on top of her. She began to pull off his shirt and kiss his neck. "I'm proud of you Sammy, of you and your gang of hillbilly hoodlums."

As they basked in the aftermath of their spontaneous love-in, Penny leaned up on one elbow.

"Where do I sign up, Sammy?"

Chapter Seven

A CASE STUDY

A fter much discussion and debate, Sammy agreed to allow Penny to accompany him on his next "outing"—against his better judgement but powerless to her persuasion.

In the meantime, between covering odd stories for the *Spring Town Gazette* and settling into a life of love with Sammy, Penny decided to write a book. In her thesis research she had been intrigued with the real-life case study of what happened on the Buffalo River. She had touched on it tangentially in her published product, but the story was so rich with tragedy, irony, and ultimately a happy ending that it warranted more. More attention, more detail, more celebration.

She would call her book *Hog Sty*. It would read like fiction but be factual at its core and serve as a beacon of hope in a world gone crazy.

The year the Buffalo River travesty began was 2012. Penny was only twelve years old and remembered nothing. But the parallels to this world she had recently returned to were striking. A beautiful river. America's first National River, so designated on March 1, 1972, by, of all people, President Richard M. Nixon. An international pork-producing conglomerate. A greedy, want-to-get-rich-quick local family. A good ol' boy system of lobbyists, legislators, regulators, and judges. A backdoor approval process that circumvented local interests and lax regulations. And, voila, a 6,500-pig CAFO alongside a major tributary to the Buffalo National River just six miles above its juncture with the mother lode. Mother Buffalo, Penny called her. Those most directly affected didn't even know until they smelled it.

It hadn't taken long for the Buffalo to begin to show the effects of effluent sprayed on surrounding fields or seeping from sewage lagoons into the groundwater through porous karst topography, as prominent local experts and scientists had predicted. Abnormally large algae blooms, fed on excess nutrients, fouled the river. There were documented cases of illness from those who canoed or swam downstream. America's first National River was under siege.

Cease and desist lawsuits languished in court, bottled up by hometown family-related judges. Opposition groups organized with support from national environmental organizations. Threats and violence flared.

By 2017, the Buffalo River had made American Rivers' top ten list of most endangered. Number nine to be exact. By 2018, it had risen to number eight. In five short years, a 6,500-pig CAFO had polluted a national treasure, with no sign of abatement or time to heal.

And then in 2019, the governor of the state of Arkansas announced a deal. The state would buy out the CAFO owners for a cool $6,000,000, partially funded by the Nature Conservancy national organization. A permanent ban on large animal production facilities in the Buffalo River watershed would be imposed. And state funds would be allocated for cleanup and restoration.

It was a fairytale ending to an all-too-common tale of corporate influence and personal greed. Not all were happy that it made millionaires out of the bad guys, but it beat the alternative and restored hope that the curative flows of nature could cleanse the damage over time.

And it was a story that deserved a larger audience in the current climate of destruction and abuse. Penny would see to it that it would be told, even cloaked in fiction to add entertainment value.

The ping of a text message caught Sammy's attention.

He tapped Penny on the shoulder, rousing her from a deep sleep.

"It's time, if you still want to play."

Penny nodded slowly and rose to throw on her newly acquired camo leggings and top. Sammy pulled his Ruger American deer rifle with the Vortex Diamondback scope from the top shelf of his closet. It was loaded and ready to fire. He dressed quickly and looked deep into Penny's eyes.

"You're sure you want to go through with this, hon? You know you really don't need to prove anything to me. I know you are on our side and taking this step just subjects you to unnecessary risk. Think about it Penny. Why—"

"It puts me on the front lines, Sammy," Penny interrupted, "which is where I want to be. Let's go."

There was an autumn chill to the dark night. Sammy's pickup clock read 1:45 a.m. They were to fire at precisely 2:30 and should be in position well before the appointed hour. He followed a rough gravel road to the edge of Johnson's property, lights off, moving ever so slowly. One of the rules he followed was to use a different access point every engagement. This one was rougher than the others he had utilized and took a little longer to traverse. He finally stopped the truck, got his bearings, and motioned for Penny to follow.

On the way out he had reviewed the process of sighting through the containment house topside curtained windows, squeezing off the five rounds his magazine would accommodate, quickly reloading, repeating, and finishing her quota before retreating swiftly to the old pickup and back to bed. He promised that the pigs were jammed in so close together she couldn't miss, even with a slightly blurred image. She nodded her understanding and winked a promise of pleasure at mission's end.

They walked slowly through a stand of woods and emerged on a small knoll looking down on the Johnson CAFO. The restless sounds of pigs stirring and snorting filled the early morning air. From their vantage point they could see more trees below and headed toward them. Sammy checked his watch. It read 2:22. They had plenty of time to spare. He had never approached the containment house from this angle, and he wanted to give Penny as easy a shot as possible, so they tried out several locations before settling on one that afforded her a clean view when she leaned out from behind the trunk of a mature Osage Orange. Penny settled into position, with Sammy crouched behind her. When his watch read 2:30, he whispered in her ear. "It's now, baby. Take your time and squeeze, firmly yet steadily."

Five quick bangs set pigs to squealing. Penny quickly reloaded as she had been taught to do and leaned out from behind the big trunk again. As she sighted in, a shot rang out. And then another.

Chapter Eight

SOLDIER DOWN

Penny had been hit. It spun her around as she cried out in pain. Someone had fired from the corner of a shed abutting the containment house. Sammy grabbed the deer rifle from her, blood dripping from her arm, and fired back. He could feel a bullet whiz by his head just as he heard the retort. This guy was serious. Sammy fired again. His second round elicited a groan.

A thud followed.

Sammy bent down and gathered the spent shell casings in one hand as he always did then scooped Penny up in his arms. She looked at him with a soft smile, which he found reassuring.

"Are you OK? Are you in pain? Where did the bastard get you?" Sammy's questions poured forth faster than blood from the wound. He clamored up the hill then literally sprinted to his truck. He laid Penny flat in the back seat of the cab, tore off his camo fleece, and wrapped a sleeve around Penny's upper arm above where blood seemed to be sourcing, pulling it tight into a knot. He turned the truck around on the rough dirt track and bounced it as fast as it would go downhill, finally finding pavement below.

He was talking to Penny the whole time, words pouring out of his mouth. She was finally able to grab a full breath and respond to his frantic questions.

"I think he got me in the arm, just above my elbow. It hurts, but your tourniquet seems to have slowed the bleeding. I'm still feeling light-headed though."

"I know a doc who I think will help. At least he is a veterinarian. That's a doctor, isn't it? Anyway, we'll go to his house. I don't think it is safe to take you to a hospital ER unless it becomes a matter of life and death. I am so sorry, Penny. Whoever it was who shot you—could have been old man Johnson himself, I guess—will pay for this. Are you still with me, Penny?"

Fifteen minutes later, Sammy was rapping on his friend Dr. Richard Bloom's front door. It took several minutes for the doctor's wife to turn on the porch light and, upon recognizing Sammy, to unbolt the lock.

"I need Richard as soon as possible," Sammy begged. "It's an emergency," he spat out, pointing to the pickup truck.

The wife, Lucinda, could only shrug. "He's not in, and I'm not sure where he is. He sometimes gets emergency calls in the middle of the night, and I've become accustomed to sleeping through them. Would you like to wait?"

Sammy nodded and retreated to his truck to pick up Penny and bring her in.

"Oh dear," Lucinda muttered. "Let's get some warm water and clean up this arm as best we can. He's usually back from these emergencies before dawn."

They stretched Penny out on the dining room table, stuck a pillow under her head, untied Sammy's fleece sleeve, and began to rub warm soapy water around the hole in her arm. She cried out in pain and briefly lost consciousness. Sammy watched in horror as Lucinda took over the heavy load. She had obviously helped Richard out before. She whispered words of comfort to Penny as consciousness returned.

Sammy heard the sound of a truck pulling up the driveway and then the squeak of a door opening. It was Richard. He too was clad in camouflage gear and carried a rifle slung over one arm.

"You're one of us, Doc? I should have known."

Richard hesitated then nodded. He moved immediately to Penny. Thirty minutes later she was sitting up, weakly sipping from a cup of hot tea. Her arm was bandaged tightly, and no blood showed through.

"So what happened, Sammy? How in the world did this come to be?"

—ww—

"Help, Sheriff, help. Jimmy's hurt bad," his wife sobbed.

"Did you call 911?"

"Yes, they're on the way, but I don't think he's going to make it," she cried. "I'm holding him best I can, but his breathing is bad."

"I'm on my way, but what happened, Maude?"

"Someone shot Jimmy while he was out checking the hogs about 2:30 or 3 this morning. He said there was at least two of the bastards, though he thought one looked kind of like a girl. Thinks he shot her from the cry he heard. All this before he passed out. I heard the ruckus, found him unconscious, and dragged him inside. He hasn't moved since."

"Stay calm, Maude. Just stay calm and hold Jimmy tight."

Minutes later the ambulance pulled up. Sheriff Silas was not far behind. The medic had to force Maude to let go of Jimmy, so they could try to treat him. Sheriff Silas arrived just in time to hear the medic whisper, "I think we've lost him, ma'am."

Maude turned toward the sheriff and fainted in his arms. The medic moved to assist her while his driver and aide lifted Jimmy's sizable carcass and placed it flat on the dining room table. When they were finally able to bring Maude around, she looked at Jimmy and flung her largess on top of him, screaming and breaking the dining room table, sending both to the floor. Sheriff could only shake his head in sadness and leave the chaos behind. He at least had one lead, albeit secondhand from a dead man. Two perpetrators, one likely female, one he likely shot and wounded, probably the lady, if that's what she can be called. He would have his team go over the whole scene in detail, but there were a couple of phone calls to make first.

"Tell me what happened, Sammy. I need to know. Who is this young lady, anyway?"

"This is my girlfriend Penny, and I stupidly put her in danger. She caught me sneaking out on one of our missions, and when I shared with her what we were up to, she wanted to be a part of it."

"You didn't even get permission from above, Sammy."

"I don't even know where 'above' is or who to ask for permission. I don't know anyone involved. I didn't know you were part of the messaging resistance. I just know I love this lady. She'll be OK, won't she?"

Richard nodded. "But I'm guessing you are in deep shit, Sammy."

Chapter Nine
SPIN

Sheriff Silas Slack's first call was to Deacon Duncan.

"Deak, Sheriff Silas here. We have a problem. There was an attack on Jimmy Johnson's hog CAFO middle of the night. Probably part of that random disruption that has been the norm for a number of months, though I haven't been into the office to receive other complaints, if any.

"So, why are you calling me, Sheriff?"

"They killed Jimmy. Shot him dead."

"Oh, I see." Deacon Duncan paused, obviously trying to process the news and, more importantly, decide what to do next. "We've got to keep this quiet, Sheriff, just like the rest of these pranksters' antics. You know what 'they' will say if we let the M-word see the light of day. This is the kind of news, particularly in the context of continuing attacks on livestock, that could make the money dry up. No more land banking; no more long-term contracts at lucrative prices; no more LLCs to pass as family farmers; no more visiting oriental angels to stoke your passion, Sheriff; no more getaways to exotic locales and locals; no more this; no more that—"

"I know, Deak, but a man has been killed and an intruder wounded. This is dangerous business, negative PR or not, and I'm obliged to enforce the law. I've got to do something, Deak, I can't just turn a deaf ear to murder. And how can you keep it out of the paper?"

"I own the damn paper, Sheriff, and you will do as I say, Silas, until you are told otherwise. First of all, you will sit down with Jimmy's wife and tell her that confidentiality is of the utmost importance in bringing these criminals to justice. That we think we know who did it but can't let out anything until we can put together our case. She will treat Jimmy's death as a freak accident. She will explain to her friends and neighbors and even the press that he got up in the middle of the night because he thought he heard an animal messing with his hogs. He had grabbed his gun and stumbled sleepily out to the confinement barns. She knew because she was following close behind. Jimmy had tripped on a shovel and fallen to the ground, discharging a round from his gun. When she had turned him over, blood was gushing from his chest. She had tried to stem the flow, but it just kept coming. He was gone shortly after the ambulance arrived."

Sheriff Silas was silent on the other end of the line.

"You will tell Maude that this is what happened. You will assure her that the murderer will be brought to justice but only if she works with us to keep this thing quiet. It is okay to grieve, it is okay to mourn, but no one must know, at least for now, how Jimmy died. Do you have it straight, Sheriff Silas?

"Yes, Deak."

"After you reach this understanding with Maude, you will call HQ and speak to the chief. You will explain in great detail what happened, how we are handling it, and why. He will applaud your calm, reasoned response. Do you understand, Sheriff Silas?"

Yes, Deak."

"And you should probably let Bottoms know as well."

"The editor of the *Spring Town Gazette?*"

"Yep. Just for the record. He won't print anything unless I tell him to."

Sheriff's next call was to a 202 area code number. "This is Sheriff Silas Slack in Spring Town, Missouri. I need to speak to the assistant secretary as soon as possible. Not his aide, just the assistant secretary himself. I am prepared to wait until you can connect me with him."

"Yes, sir, Sheriff Slack, I think you said? I'm on it."

—⟆⟆—

"So, what do we do next, Sammy?"

"I would suggest making love, but that might be a little difficult in the state you are in."

This brought a brief smile to Penny's face, followed by a grimace. Her left arm was bandaged and tucked into a sling. They sat on the old couch in front of their TV, nervously watching the midday news to see how their early morning shoot-out might be covered. There was no mention of it. Same for evening news and the 10 p.m. report. Not a single word.

"I know I hit the bastard. I heard him grunt and thud on the ground. Surely he reported it all to the sheriff's office? I just hope they don't find any of your blood on the ground. I tried to stir it into the dirt as best I could, but it was all happening so fast."

"Maybe they will have something in the morning *Spring Town Gazette*? Oh shit, I forgot. I'm supposed to check in for my column assignment tomorrow morning at nine. How can I go in looking like this? How can I type a column? What do I tell my editor I did to myself?

"I'd say you call in sick, get his assignment over the phone, and dictate your column to me. I'm not a great typist and it will probably take me a while, but I can get it done and to him before the day is over. I don't know what else to tell you, Penny."

Next day Penny was on the phone with her editor, explaining her illness. Bernard Bottoms, her editor, was irked. "What do you mean you can't come in?"

Bernard Bottoms was nothing more than a company shill. He did what *Spring Town Gazette* majority owner Deacon Duncan wanted and approved, and he published only what Duncan wanted published. If Herr Duncan said "write it," Bernard did. If he said "scratch it," Bernard did. There was not room for independent thinking in the newsroom of the *Spring Town Gazette*.

Penny had noticed that a number of her past columns had been edited, toned down, or pumped up, depending on the nature of her message. She hadn't thought much about it because she was only allowed to tackle milquetoast issues. A new small business in town? The crazy weather in the Ozarks? The beginning of a new school year? And then there was the marriage of Daisy Mae Pinochle to Donny Dan Cribbage. She had actually made a joke about the "games people play," which was stricken from final copy. (She found out later that the Cribbages were pig CAFO folks.) An increase in parking meter fees to fund much-needed capital improvements? She had complained about that, but her protest had been removed. The discovery of an albino squirrel trapped in a city park trash barrel? Her clever observation of "reverse racism in Spring Town" was quickly whited out.

Penny had asked permission to research and write about water quality issues. Things like faint odors in drinking water, water table degradation, and the like but was turned down. "People aren't interested in that shit," Editor Bottoms loudly proclaimed. "They are if your water smells like it," Penny had responded. "I said no, *no*," ended the conversation, with an implied threat that her job depended on it.

But Penny plugged along, carefully hoeing the editor's line, just happy to have a writing job of any nature. She figured *Hog Sty* would ultimately get her fired but soldiered on in the interim, with both her day job and her book project.

Penny finally negotiated a sick day off if she promised to e-mail the editor his copy by 4 p.m. "Anything exciting in the news this morning, Mr. Bottoms?" Penny had asked in passing. The negative reply she had received surprised her. She finished her Sammy-typed column on fall colors before noon and promised she would be in the following week and on call if her editor needed her.

When she and Sammy determined that there was no mention of their shoot-out in either of the next two dailies, they grew suspicious. And then a short obituary for beloved civic leader Jimmy Johnson, victim of a firearms accident, set red flags to waving.

"You mean the fat bastard is dead?"

"Could you have killed him?"

"I hope to hell not."

Sheriff Silas and his two deputies scoured the rise above Jimmy Johnson's hog CAFO, looking for any clues as to who might have murdered him. They found a few blurred shoe tracks but nothing else. No spent shell casings, no sign of blood, no articles of clothing.

They visited every doctor in town and the local hospital emergency room. Nothing. No reports of wounded civilians, strange visitors the night of the killing, or really anything out of the ordinary. Whoever had committed this dastardly crime was clearly a professional.

The sheriff did confirm that there had been reports from the usual suspects about livestock assassinations the night of the murder but no confirmed sightings or apprehensions of suspects.

And, finally, Deak had been correct. The assistant secretary praised the sheriff roundly for his calm and measured handling of the incident. He even promised to reward him later in the month, with cash and a long weekend in St. Louis with several "playmates" from home base. Deacon Duncan handled the arrangements, paid the bills, and even joined him in the frolic. All under the guise of a pig bureau informational meeting on expanding pork production in the interest of securing additional international market niches. Wives were excluded from these sessions because of the technical nature of the presentations.

Chapter Ten

DIGGING DEEPER

P enny was flabbergasted over the lack of coverage related to the death of Jimmy Johnson. One simple obit, a firearms accident, a grieving wife, and nothing more.

Sammy was despondent. He may have killed a man? He might never find out? Was this a good thing or a bad thing? If he had killed Jimmy, he could go to jail. No one in this crazy town would ever believe that he fired in self-defense. And that bothered him too. Did he? Could he and Penny have slipped away and left CAFO Man to his pigs and own devices? And then he remembered the bullet that had whizzed by his head. So close he felt the air move. The man had shot Penny and was trying to kill him. They never once fired his way until he fired on them first. If that wasn't the definition of self-defense, what was? That Penny agreed with him provided only passing comfort.

As they sat quietly over coffee the phone rang. Sammy answered. It was the damn editor, Bernard Bottoms, and he needed to speak with Penny as soon as possible.

"Ms. Plumb?"

"Yes, and it's Plum. No 'b' sound on the end."

"Whatever. I need you down here immediately to report on a developing story. I need to guide you through our purpose in publishing it before you take it on. It deals with some sensitive issues regarding privacy that we need to respect. I wouldn't touch it at all except that word of mouth is moving it through the community quickly. So, get down here. Now."

Penny looked at her bandaged arm, still resting in a sling. "I'm still not 100%, Mr. Bottoms."

"Doesn't matter. I just need a body that can listen and write. You can do that, I suppose?"

"I'll be there soon."

Penny looked at Sammy. "What do I tell him about this?" she asked, cradling her wounded arm after removing the sling? "Probably a good idea to leave this behind," she added before throwing the sling on the kitchen table.

—⋙—

The story Bottoms needed Penny to cover so desperately was in fact pretty mundane. Some local state pol was dedicating a bridge early in the afternoon to a deceased relative. Penny couldn't begin to discern what was sensitive about the whole thing.

"So, what did you do to your arm, Plumb?"

"Nothing major, Mr. Bottoms. And, it's Plum, without the 'b' sound on the end."

"It looks kind of serious," he added, leaning in more closely before lightly touching. "Almost looks like a wound or something? Your live-in stab you? Or shoot you?"

"No, Mr. Bottoms. Nothing like that," Penny responded, trying to hide her grimace.

"Sensitive to the touch, huh, Plumb?"

"Speaking of sensitive, you want me to drive out in the country and cover this bridge dedication? What is so sensitive about that, to use your own words?"

"Well, the name that will go on the bridge belonged to a cousin of the dedicating politician, who had an affair with the politician's wife not long before he passed. Everyone in town knows about it and what a philanderer he was. Several community leaders had, shall we say, similar fates befall their mates. Most kept it quiet, though one divorced. He had a penchant for disrupting the rich and powerful."

"Kind of a bedroom Robin Hood," Penny quipped and managed a laugh.

Bottoms didn't. "Just cover the story, Plumb, tastefully, respectfully, within the rails of good journalism."

"So, why the naming recognition, with all this sleeping around?"

"Money. Cold, hard currency. The man was a major under-the-table contributor to the governor and never slept with his wife. Again, all I am saying is be brief and professional, just don't lay it on too thick about the state rep and his cousin. Five hundred words and two photos will do. Can you handle that?"

"Yes, sir, Mr. Bottoms, yes, sir."

Penny headed out toward the new bridge and thought she recognized the road as the one she and Sammy had taken on their way to the pig CAFO, the one that had changed their destiny. She then passed a road sign bearing the name of the deceased and knew it was. A chill crept up her back and through her wound.

After the bridge dedication and celebratory photos, she headed back toward the office, passing the marked road, then stopping, reversing, and turning in. She knew better but lost that battle to her innate sense of curiosity. She pulled up to a large brick house with the pig CAFO splayed out behind it. She even thought she recognized the sheltered knoll from which they had fired.

Guess one just gets used to the smell, particularly if the money is rolling in, she thought to herself.

A heavyset lady walked out the front door and motioned for her to come forward. Penny obliged, exited her car, walked toward the door, and extended her hand. She mentioned the tribute that her paper had run in honor of the woman's husband and added that she had just wanted to express her condolences in person. The woman leaked tears but invited her in to sit for a visit.

"I get so lonely these days," she said. "I miss Jimmy so much, and no one ever stops by. I'm left with the pigs, a couple of Mexicans to work them, and the memories. I just do what the company tells me to when their vet stops by to medicate and assess weights. They will soon be shipping this batch off and bringing in a new one to fatten up. I'm just so alone out here." The leaking turned to full-fledged sobbing.

"I'm sorry, Mrs. Johnson, so sorry."

"I just wish they would catch the ones who did this awful thing. That would at least bring me some peace at night."

Penny couldn't believe what she had just heard. "Did you say who did this awful thing, Mrs. Johnson?"

"No, no. ... I misspoke. It was all a big accident. Please don't pay any attention to me, dear. I'm just a lonely, distraught old lady who can't keep her stories straight. Please forgive me. What did you say your name is, by the way?"

Penny hesitated a moment before responding. "Ruth. Ruth Moseley."

"And you work for that paper, the *Gazette*?"

"Occasionally."

—⁂—

Penny couldn't get home to Sammy fast enough.

"You did what? You went back to the farm where you got shot? What were you thinking, Penny?"

"I don't know, Sammy. It was just on impulse. And there is more. Mrs. Johnson let slip a comment I don't think she intended. She said she hoped they 'catch the ones who did this awful thing,' or something like that. She quickly restated, excusing herself for being an old lady who 'couldn't keep her stories straight.' They know, Sammy. They know it was murder, and they used the word 'ones,' so they know it was more than one of us. And they are covering it up. Why, Sammy, why are they doing it?"

"I killed a man, Penny. And just when I talk myself into self-defense, you up and use the word 'murder.'" Sammy sobbed.

"I'm sorry, Sammy, she didn't use that word. But that's what they think. I still don't understand why the cover-up? Makes no sense. You would think they would want an all-points bulletin out or something like that. Everyone in town looking for suspects. But no. Just denial. I bet Bottoms knows. There is something going on here that is bigger than you and me, Sammy, and we are caught up right in the middle of it."

Chapter Eleven

DEEP DOO DOO

"So, what were you doing out at the Johnson's farm, Plumb?" Bottoms asked when Penny checked in to file her "sensitive" bridge dedication story.

Penny looked confused as Bottoms continued.

"Maude Johnson just called me to tell me about the sweet young lady by the name of Ruth who had stopped by to personally share the *Gazette's* condolences. We have never had a Ruth in this office and the physical description she provided was you, complete with bandaged arm. What were you doing out there, Plumb? That was not part of your assignment, and you know how particular I am about doing no more that you are asked to. What were you up to and why an alias?"

"I just recognized the name on the road sign and wanted to tell Mrs. Johnson how sorry we are. You certainly wrote a beautiful obit on her husband. I thought you would be grateful to me for generating goodwill for the paper in the community?"

"Why the fake name, Plumb? What are you hiding?"

"Nothing. Again, just wanting the *Spring Town Gazette* to get credit, not me. Actually, I didn't even think about it. It just popped out. I figured that a few kind words to a lady in mourning might bring a smile and no more. I didn't know she would call you."

"Obviously. Did she tell you anything else? Like about her husband. Or the accident. Did she talk about that at all?"

Penny found herself briefly hesitating before answering, "No. Just the normal pleasantries."

"OK, Plumb, just finish your story and get out of here. And don't ever do anything like this again. Got it?"

"Yes, sir, and the name is Plum, without the 'b' sound at the end," Penny said as she sat down at in her cubicle. Thankfully there was no one else around as the process of putting 500 words together and scanning two phone images was slow and painful for her. She typed most everything with the index finger of her left hand before submitting the whole piece by e-mail to her editor. She had been properly deceitful, so he should make very few changes.

—⁕—

That evening as she and Sammy sat trying to wrap their brains around what they had learned from Maude Johnson about covering up her husband's true cause of death, the phone rang. It was the vet who had worked on Penny's arm, Richard Bloom.

"Sammy, I need to visit with you as soon as possible. There are things going on that I believe you need to be aware of. Can I stop by tonight?"

"Of course, Richard. Any time. We are in all evening. Is everything OK?"

"Lucy and I will be by in an hour."

—⁕—

Deep in the Mark Twain National Forest, leaves stirred as a figure slipped through the undergrowth. And then a second, third, and fourth. All removed their rudimentary garments and jumped or waded into Goose Creek to cool down. A man, a women, and two young children frolicked and splashed in the cleansing waters for over an hour before drying off with old flea-bitten towels and redressing. This was their bathing hole, no one else's, far upstream from where most entered or observed the creek. The log shelter they had constructed and expanded over time was only five minutes away, up a steep hill and buried deep in tall trees, safe from water's spring rise and human interaction. The paradise they had escaped to from a world going mad, in the two adult's eyes, was a holy sanctuary, grounded in love of nature and each other, rooted in solid ground. This was their statement of right and wrong.

Nor were they alone in their pursuit of life, liberty, and happiness.

—⟋⟍—

"OK, you two," Richard began. "You have really stirred up a hornet's nest with your little adventure. I have gotten word through the usual channels that I am to pass to you. Lay low for a while. I explained that you fired in self-defense, only after Penny was shot and you felt a bullet whiz by your head, but they are still upset that a man has been killed. Beyond blame, they are pissed that you, Sammy, invited an unauthorized accomplice into the network without higher approval and that it ended with a death. So, you are benched for a while for your behavior and your safety.

"Who are 'they,' Richard?"

"I couldn't tell you if I even knew, Sammy. Just know that they have organized the whole local resistance to CAFO and corporate farming abuses. Their—and our—clandestine efforts have done little to stem the tide, but this killing is bringing powerful forces to bear on our efforts to message and disrupt."

"So, why have they worked so hard to cover up the shooting rather than engage the community in apprehending the perpetrators, namely us?"

"Well, if you mean the other 'they', there seems to be almost a paranoia about any speck of negative news, like CAFO animal shootings and now a perceived murder, reaching the media. Our region is evidently represented to international mega-conglomerate corporate agriculture as a safe haven for unbridled expansion, land acquisition, money laundering, and profiteering. I'm told that outside forces have been recruited to assist the sheriff in tracking you two down and that strangers were observed combing the entire area surrounding the Johnson CAFO just two days ago. Local news coverage is on lockdown, which is possible because some guy named Deacon something owns the paper, controls the editor, and influences local TV programming."

"I can attest to that," Penny said with a nod. "I work for the bastard, the editor that is. If I veer outside the guardrails in my reporting or writing, I get my hand slapped."

"Speaking of which, how is your arm, Penny?"

"It hurts like hell, Dr. Richard, to be honest. I had to give up my sling today so that Mr. Bottoms wouldn't get too suspicious of my injury. I typed a whole column for tomorrow's paper

with my left hand while trying to rest my bad arm on the desk and look natural."

"Let me take a look," ordered Richard. With Lucy's help, he unbound the bandage and grimaced at what he saw. "It looks infected, Penny, I've got to get some antibiotic in you as soon as possible or you'll have to visit the ER, which most certainly is being watched closely. Can you come back to my place right now, so I can IV you? This doesn't look good."

"Let's go," said Sammy. "We can talk later. All of these 'theys' have twisted my mind in knots. Good theys, bad theys, and us in the middle. Of what?"

"We will, Sammy. Just know that for now you are off the contact list, and you are to engage in no activities which might get you busted. We are all at risk through you."

Chapter Twelve

BIDING TIME

Threatened offices of the *Spring Town Gazette* were small and crowded. The only private area was Mr. 'sBottoms' office, which he kept closed and locked most of the time. In addition to Penny, there were two part-time writers and a secretary. Rarely was there more than one person around at any one time. It was a quiet place, foregoing stimulating newsroom chatter for a sense of dread and dead.

Copy for the next day's paper was due to Mr. Bottoms by 4 p.m. for his approval, before his secretary forwarded it to a sub-contractor for printing and distribution. Unlike other midsize town papers that had failed by the dozens, if not hundreds, the *Gazette* didn't need to worry about relevant content, circulation numbers, online readers, or even survival. It was a propaganda machine protected by wealthy interests tied to corporate agriculture.

Penny longed to get a peek into Bottoms' office. Her reporter's instincts screamed to her that the answers to a lot of the new questions defining her life with Sammy lay within. She began to walk in with trivial requests whenever he was in. The result was always the same. Penny would knock on the door. No response, though she knew he was in there. She would knock again.

"Who is it and what do you want? Can't you tell that I'm busy?"

"It's Penny Plum, Mr. Bottoms, and I have a question for you."

"Okay, Plumb, ask it."

"The name is Plum, without the 'b' sound, sir, and I require a visual aid to accurately pose my inquiry."

"Okay, Plumb, come on in."

And it seemed to always end the same. Penny would sit down in front of his desk, thrust a photo she had taken in front of him, and ask his assessment. While Bottoms studied the photo, Penny would study his office. To the right and left of his desk were bookshelves, filled mostly with bizarre publications and photographs taken with right-wing politicians. Directly behind him loomed a tall file cabinet with open padlocks on it, implying usage. No doubt it was locked down tight and alarmed when he wasn't there, as was his office. There were generally manilla file folders on the desk in front of him, which he made a point of slamming shut when Penny sat down. There were no personal or family photos on the desk, despite him being a husband and father. Weird guy with many secrets was about the best Penny could deduce. If only she could get into some of those files from the cabinet. Who knows what secrets she would find?

After a week of such observations, Penny finally gave up, reconciled to the fact that she would never be able to penetrate the security shield that Bottoms had erected around his office and his life. Between laying low, as she and Sammy were ordered to do, and her slow recovery from her wound infection, Penny's restless spirit began to eat at her. She had to do something to shed light on the great cover-up, but she didn't have a clue what that might be.

One late afternoon, while she was working on her weekly column, which was not yet due, she thought she heard a distinct thud. She looked around, knowing that the secretary had gone home after submitting copy for the next day's paper and that she was alone, unless Bottoms was still in his office. So, it must have been Bottoms.

She arose, crossed the floor, and knocked on his door. No answer, as usual. She knocked again, expecting an irritated response. There was none. She tapped for the third time and turned the doorknob. She was stunned with the scene that presented.

Bottoms was lying prostrate on the floor, blank face toward the ceiling. Several files were strewn on the floor around him. She tried to focus on his face to ascertain his condition but was drawn back to several 8 x 10 photos of men and naked women in various stages of interaction. She rushed to Bottoms and checked for pulse, for breathing, for eye movement. She found none of the above. She glanced up and behind his chair to the open file cabinet. What in the hell do I do now, she asked out loud to no one but the dead soldier in front of her.

Penny's first instinct was to all 911 and bring in an ambulance crew to confirm Bottoms' death. Instead she called Sammy and asked him to meet her at the office immediately. That it was urgent. She knew Bottoms couldn't be helped. She also knew that she would likely never have access again to the treasure trove behind his desk, a potential mother lode of information that might save her and Sammy from persecution, prosecution, or even incarceration. The choice was easy in the end. She and Sammy over a dead bastard.

"Sammy, I need you now. Bring some of those thin plastic gloves under the sink."

"Why?"

"Don't ask. Just get here as fast as you can."

Sammy was there knocking on the front door twelve minutes later. She locked up behind him, strapped on the gloves to both hands, led the way into Bottoms' office, and locked that door as well. The office had no windows, which she really hadn't noticed before, so there was no need to pull shades or dim lights.

"Whoa. Doesn't this creep you out, hon?" whispered Sammy, staring at the lifeless body in front of him.

"Not as much as the thought of us going to jail for the rest of our lives."

An hour later, Penny and Sammy emerged from their illicit cocoon of dirty secrets carrying a stack of folders. During that time they had gone through the whole file cabinet, as well as Bottoms' desk drawers. Penny's investigative reporter instincts guided her scan of files and documents and helped her focus on finding an underlying story line. They grabbed the file on Bottoms' desk labeled **CURRENT** as an afterthought, then carefully covered up their intrusion, aligning remaining folders with precision, closing some file drawers and padlocking them, shutting desk drawers, and leaving office lights on.

They left what remained of Bottoms sprawled as he had fallen and reasoned that they should leave things as if he had been working when stricken, office door unlocked. Whoever opened in the morning was going to be in for a big surprise.

Deacon Duncan and Sheriff Silas thoroughly enjoyed their long weekend in St. Louis at the "pig bureau" workshop. And about the only work that was done was by the five Asian ladies who had been shipped in specifically for the purpose of pleasuring their two special guests.

The actual location of the "workshop" was a resort community an hour from the airport. The A-frame they were housed in was secluded, rustic, and loaded with expensive food and wine, in addition to the exotic entertainment.

"Nice to be on the payroll, isn't it, Sheriff?" quipped Deacon.

Sheriff Silas Slack could only smile and nod his agreement over his bare fat belly.

Chapter Thirteen

TREASURE TROVE

P enny and Sammy couldn't wait to delve more carefully into the files they had filched. One in particular caught their attention. It was thick, bound, and entitled in large bold typed letters:

CLASSIFIED: TOP SECRET
UNITED STATES DEPARTMENT OF AGRICULTURE
DEEP AG, THE 51st STATE—A Vision of the Future

It would take time to review, so they laid it aside until they could sort through the rest and develop context for their discovery.

Two of the files contained photos of men in compromising situations and positions with women, mostly Asian, but some of darker skin, perhaps Hispanic. Penny recognized some of the men from her local reporting beat.

"That's the mayor." She laughed out loud. "Wish I could run this one in tomorrow's *Gazette*." Maybe she could was an afterthought she shrugged off as unrealistic. The mayor was seated in a bath of soapy water being sponged down by three totally naked ladies. Each appeared to be of Asian heritage.

"The guy with the sheriff's hat on must be the sheriff, don't you think, Penny? And the bare-naked lady on his lap does not appear to be under arrest for indecent exposure, best as I can tell," added Sammy. "Not bad. . . .—"

"Shut up, Sammy. There are at least two dozen different men in compromising positions in this file alone. I bet they are all connected to politics or local governance."

"Or pig CAFOs, or 'Pork Capital of the World.'"

"You are right, Sammy. That one right there bears a striking resemblance to the obit photo of family man and farmer Jimmy Johnson. Poor old Maude. Little did she know, or she would not be missing the sorry bastard. Family farmer, my ass."

"Penny, I've never heard you talk like that before. Just what do you say about me behind my back?"

This set both of them to laughing out loud.

"This one is particularly disgusting," muttered Sammy. "The little girl couldn't be much older than fourteen or fifteen years old. And look what the fat guy is making her do."

"I recognize him, too, from the bridge dedication. He made one of the short congratulatory speeches. Missed his name. Disgusting is right. Make that, this just isn't right. What a treasure trove of bribery materials. Can you imagine if any of these photos ever got out? And here they are—or were—in the hands of the local newspaper editor, with instant access to public dissemination. Talk about keeping the flock in lockstep with the party line? And now we have them."

They put aside the smut and moved on. There were copies of checks, big checks, six figure checks. Many were made out to limited liability corporations, political campaigns, and industry groups. Some even had politicians' names on them. "Committee to Re-elect Birdbrain Butthole." "Committee for Profitable Agriculture." "Pigs for President Porker"

"It doesn't say that, Penny."

"Might as well."

Three hours and maybe thirty files later, Sammy said "I'm hungry. I've got to have something to eat." Something they had forgotten to do in their rush to review.

As they sat around chewing on the burgers and fries Sammy had ordered in, Penny observed, "You know this hamburger meat comes from a CAFO, Sammy?"

"Yep, but likely not one around here. Probably West Texas or Kansas or someplace that's ruined already. Besides, it tastes good."

"Some would say that about the Ozarks, you know. Ruined, that is."

"But CAFOs don't belong here. They ruin our water."

"And our water-based economy. Just look around and then eat another pork chop."

"What do you want me to eat. Tofu chops?"

"Hypocrite."

The trip through Bottoms' collection of incendiary information had left them breathless. And tired. They decided to sleep on it and finish the next day. Penny likely wouldn't be asked to cover Bottoms' demise. "Wonder if they will even admit he is gone?"

"Might even prop his sorry carcass up in his chair and pickle it," Sammy said with a laugh.

"Goodnight, Sammy. We'll finish things up tomorrow and figure out what to do next."

The next morning dawned warm yet fall-like. Colors were bursting out all over the Ozarks. Golds, reds, browns, muted greens. The landscape was a patchwork quilt of color, all framed in a shower of falling leaves. Sammy and Penny took a short walk in the wonderland before getting back to business. They wondered if Bottoms' body had been found yet.

More files, more incriminating photos, more bank records and check stubs. Really too much to absorb at one time. There was enough stuff in these files to flush out the corruption that had spread like a cancer in their community and region, just not enough jail cells to house the predators.

About midday, they reached the bottom of the pile. The twelve o'clock news had no mention of Bottoms' demise, which set them to wondering if he would just disappear into an innocuous accident like Jimmy Johnson.

"Guess it's time to get into this thing that almost looks like a manifesto of sorts. 'Deep Ag?' 'Vision?' What do you suppose, Sammy?"

"Let's finish this out before we go there, Penny. There are a couple more."

"Just the same old disgusting crap, Sammy. But OK. Wait. Look at this on one the bottom. I remember grabbing it as we walked out from the top of Bottoms' desk. Wonder what in the world it is all about?"

The file marked **CURRENT** stopped them in their tracks. It was evidently Bottoms' *plat de jour* and represented what was next on his agenda. Penny glanced at his handwritten notes and was shocked to find her name about halfway down the first page: "Follow up on suspicions about Plumb with Sheriff Silas when he returns from his romp."

"Say what?" screamed Penny. "What suspicions? And it's Plum without the 'b,' shithead."

Chapter Fourteen

SAY WHAT?

S ay what, again," sobbed Penny, not quite so loudly. Sammy looked on in stunned silence.

"They know, Sammy. The bad 'theys' know it was us"

"Calm down, Penny. Know what? They have no evidence."

"They know my arm was injured, and Bottoms even suggested a gunshot wound to me at one point. They know I was snooping around the Johnsons' CAFO and using an alias."

"It's all circumstantial, hon. They have no hard evidence, no shell casings, no eyewitness except a dead man. They have no motive. They have nothing."

"They have a hometown justice system with a crooked sheriff and partial judges and juries that don't require hard evidence. I think we ought to make a run for it, Sammy."

"For what, Penny? I think we're the ones who have the hard evidence and that we might have even more if we can work our way through this last file folder."

Little did Penny and Sammy know what awaited them.

Sheriff Silas Slack began to sort through his mail. He would move to his computer to check e-mails once all the paper crap was thrown away.

He was still smiling over his long weekend getaway, courtesy of the state pig bureau and their sponsors, whoever they were. He just knew that he didn't want to know. He was grateful for the lifestyle his position and his benefactors, near and halfway around the world, afforded him. Where else would a middle-aged, overweight, underachieving white guy be personally tended to by the most exotic ladies in the world, as if they really liked and wanted him.

Sheriff Silas had fallen into this gig almost by accident. He had grown up poor in rural Missouri, son of a struggling multigenerational family farming family, with barely enough to eat and wear on his back and feet. If there was one thing he had promised himself as a young man, it was that he would never ever set foot on another small family farm except to evict the ignorant, sorry practitioners. This founding character principle really left him only two reasonable career paths. Small-town banking? Small-town law enforcement? He could either foreclose or evict. And since he wasn't very good at math or manners, sheriff or police chief sounded like the logical alternative.

When Silas Slack graduated high school, he fled his sorry small town, leaving his impoverished family to sink deeper in debt. He also left behind the pretty little high school sophomore he had impregnated by accident.

He had taken the bus to St. Louis, befriended an elderly, kind of senile acting gentleman along the way, who offered to help him get settled in the big city. Silas had bedazzled him with his altruistic vision of a career in law enforcement, and the man had recently retired from the St. Louis County Sheriff's Office. He promised to open doors and grease skids to jump-start Silas's training. He even gave Silas a $100 bill and the address of a boarding house that would take him in until he could get on his feet. Silas figured it was about time he got lucky this way, having had to scrape by with nothing all his life.

Silas passed through his entry-level training quickly and efficiently and was soon wearing the badge of an officer. He particularly endeared himself to his immediate supervisor by not putting up with any shit from black folks. In that much of his time was spent in north St. Louis County, he had ample opportunity to prove himself. He crossed the human decency—and probably legal—line a time or two but had plenty of help covering tracks and advanced rapidly in the ranks. He was kind to the old man who had helped give him a chance and mourned his descent into dementia. At least enough to say goodbye to him and repay the $100.

One day his supervisor approached him with an opportunity. One of his closest friends from training times was the current sheriff in Spring Town, Missouri, who was looking for a proven senior deputy. In that the sheriff would be of retirement age in two years, it would likely offer young Silas an outstanding opportunity for upward mobility. Sadly, there weren't that many people of color to horse around, but he was certain Silas could find another constituency to endear himself to and build his credentials on.

It didn't take long for Silas to say yes and start building.

Spring Town was in a state of agricultural consolidation. Once a mecca of small farms, dairy, pork, chicken, with a prosperous water-based recreational economy, someone or something had put a big bullseye on the Ozarks. Cheap land, plentiful water, lax regulation screamed opportunity to corporate ag. Get big or get out they challenged and began to buy or merge, utilizing local front people, while retaining controlling interest. All under the guise of "right to farm" and giving family farmers the tools to survive. Limited liability companies were their vehicles of choice. Senior Deputy Sheriff Slack sensed the potential in this transition quickly. He could become part of this consolidation and reap the benefits or just sit by and watch it happen. He chose the former and began to build a reputation as a crusading law enforcement officer bent on something he had always dreamed of: putting small penny-ante family farms out of business.

His boss was less comfortable with what was happening and opted to retire earlier than planned. He installed Slack as his interim successor and supported him in his first victorious election. He then moved on to a less tumultuous section of the country, cautioning Sheriff Silas Slack in parting, "Watch out. There's people out there trying to buy you. There's people out there trying to sell you. Be sure and remember the difference." Sheriff Silas had thought it was good advice back then and still did. He played at both ends of the spectrum. The "eviction sheriff," as he became known, had found his niche in the new economy and prosperity. Along the way he picked up a good but heavyset wife, who bore him a pair of daughters. He would have preferred sons but was certain that his daughters would make good but heavyset wives someday and might fetch him a dowry of some value. Maybe even a stake in a hog CAFO, for all he knew.

The sheriff finished rifling through the stacks of wasted stamps and paper and moved on to the electronic exchanges that awaited his response. As he opened up his e-mail account, his newly appointed deputy burst through the closed door to his office without knocking. Slack quickly shut the folder he had been smiling at on his desk, the one that contained the weekend's 8 x 10 photos for him to look back on and forward to at the same time. He kind of felt like he had fallen in love with the voluptuous young thing that had satisfied his every need and was enjoying staring at her naked body straddling his lap. But he knew in his heart there would be another one just like her next time.

"Sheriff Silas, Bottoms is dead. They found him in his office, sprawled on the floor. Probably a heart attack, but we need to rule out foul play. Let's go."

The sheriff felt neither sadness nor surprise. It was that kind of world these days. A far cry from where he had come.

Chapter Fifteen

DEEP AG,
THE FIFTY-FIRST STATE

Penny sat staring at the bound document, Sammy looking over her shoulder.

CLASSIFIED: TOP SECRET
UNITED STATES DEPARTMENT OF AGRICULTURE
(USDA)
DEEP AG, THE 51st STATE—A Coalition for Prosperity
with a Vision for the Future

She opened the file slowly and began thumbing through page by page. The "Vision Statement" up front seemed to say it all:

"The Coalition for Prosperity envisions a world in which most are fed, a few get very wealthy, and we control the flow of goods and money."

It was translated into Chinese and Portuguese directly below. The signatories included the United States Department of Agriculture, the Chinese Ministry of Agriculture and Rural Affairs, and the Brazilian Ministry of Agriculture, Livestock, and Supply. Also signing were four multinational corporate partners

The document went on to delineate an intricate web of interconnections between the three governments, or parts thereof, and the four corporate agricultural conglomerates that controlled most meat production in the world. It spelled out secret trading agreements and tariff exemptions that superseded published arrangements and payment mechanisms that flowed through offshore banks, beyond the scrutiny of regulators and currency controls. And this was just Section One of the document. Neither Penny nor Sammy could quite grasp the enormity of it all.

Section Two delineated operational infrastructure, from the assistant secretary or director or vice president of each of the seven signatories down the chain of command to ground-level implementation. It was not clear whether presidents of countries or corporations, or other high-ranking officials of either, were privy to the plot, wished to stay clear of it, or were just ignoring it.

Section Three identified potentially lucrative target markets for development and expansion. Penny and Sammy could easily identify the Missouri-Arkansas Ozarks on this prospect list. There were at least twenty more regions in the United States alone and hundreds in China. The Amazon rain forest represented Brazil's land of opportunity for clearing and commercial agricultural development. CAFOs were the identified expansion vehicles of choice.

Section Four followed the money. From local currencies through middlemen and lobbyists to local politicians and civic leaders to state legislators and governors to corporate sponsors, integrators, and investors to offshore financial institutions ...and back. A giant circle of influence peddling, financial meddling, and Big Ag coddling. The philosophy was simple enough that even Penny and Sammy could digest it. Buy out local farmers in targeted regions around the world under threat of forcing them out of business, pay for land and patronage, capture market share, fix prices, co-opt corrupt lawmakers into softening or eliminating regulations, particularly as regards environmental protections, and pocket all the change. Of which there was a lot.

Section Five got down in the weeds regarding bribes, kickbacks, sexual favors, and the like.

In that the entire system from the ground up would be built for and around select men, it was only logical to provide a vast network of prostitutes to reward loyalty and close deals. Clandestine sub-contractors in each country would provide supply to fulfill participants' demand. Principally Asian women to investors and partners in the U.S., Hispanic in China, and Black and mixed race to all. Section Five also detailed funding sources and payment intermediaries.

Section Six provided financial forecasts of the effect of this massive reapportionment of financial resources on world markets and individual fortunes.

At least this was how Penny summed it up in her head and shared with Sammy.

"Two hundred pages of visions, plans, numbers, charts, and logistics condensed to half a dozen paragraphs. It's the only way that I can even start to grasp it, Sammy. My summary doesn't begin to do justice to the depth and breadth of this international agribusiness conspiracy, but you get the picture. This is big business, with a capital B, Sammy, and it has led to the changes and environmental deterioration we have witnessed in the Ozarks. This is vast, it is evil, it is manipulating the lives of many to grow the fortunes of a few, and in the end, it will destroy our planet as we know it."

"So, what do we do now, Penny? Where do we go next?"

"I don't know, Sammy. I just don't know. We do have to get all of this evidence of a clandestine international conspiracy in safe hands as soon as possible. Preferably with someone or some organization that can assimilate and understand it all well enough to bring daylight to it and stand up to what is going on. I do know that this is our ticket to freedom if the powers that be decide to take us out. We cannot afford to lose it."

Deacon Duncan was already at Bottoms' office by the time Sheriff Silas and his deputy arrived.

Deacon sat praying over the stiff cadaver in his capacity as an elder of the True Church of Christ.

The others bent to one knee to join in his exhortations that Bernard Bottoms find a happy home in heaven.

After the last "Amen," Deacon pulled Sheriff Silas aside for a brief discussion.

"Well, our regional leadership team is down to two, Sheriff. You and me. And we have decisions to make. As previously structured, I felt we functioned fairly efficiently. I developed the ground game, you enforced it, and Bottoms kept the records. Only fitting that the editor of the newspaper that we own kept all the dirt under lock and key, a veiled threat to anyone who might wish to opt out or tell all. With Bottoms gone we need a new repository for such damning information. Any suggestions? That's question one. Question two involves whether we wish to hint at foul play in Bottoms' death. My inclination is no for the same reasons we covered up Jimmy Johnson's murder and the periodic hits on CAFO animals. Bad news is bad business. And, finally, how do we secure and protect all of the information Bottoms has accumulated over the years? Frankly, I don't even know what is in the files he has padlocked in his office. I gave up trying to keep track long ago. For all I know, the bastard has shit on me, and you, that we probably need to get rid of. Who can we trust to go through his archives and preserve the information vital to our continuing operations while protecting ourselves? Any thoughts on any of this?"

"Maybe HQ will have a suggestion on replacing Bottoms and his indispensable role as keeper of records and director of smut," sheriff said with a chuckle.

"Good idea, Sheriff. We'll report in to the assistant secretary's office as soon as we secure the area."

"I totally agree with the 'natural death' theory. It doesn't hurt to tell the truth now and again does it, Deak." Sheriff laughed. "As for reviewing and cataloguing the archives, why not leave that to me? I'm leery of bringing someone in from the outside to dredge up our dirty little secrets, aren't you? Not sure what I will find, keep, or shred, but at least it's me making the call. I will of course run anything problematic by you. I can seal off the office under the guise of securing Bottoms' papers for his family and spend the next couple of days going through everything. Will have it cleaned up for whomever is coming next, as well as safe for us."

After their call to the assistant secretary's office, Sheriff Silas headed back to his own to process his e-mails. They were ordinary, run-of-the-mill, for the most part, including a heart emoji from the young lady who had so smitten him over the weekend. Maybe he would get to see her again. He started to e-mail her that he hoped so but decided not to. Better not get too personal with an exotic hooker.

Up next was a short note from Bernard Bottoms, obviously written before he crashed over. Sheriff read it once then again. It caused Sheriff Silas's skin to bristle.

"Sheriff, I have a funny feeling about this young lady who works in my office. Her name is Plumb and she is a beat writer. She has this injury to her arm that she is reluctant to discuss. It seems more serious than she lets on. And, she was snooping around out at widow Johnson's place last week, using an alias of all things. What did Johnson tell Maude before he passed? He thought there were two of them and that he heard one yelp when he shot? Could it have been her? Could her live-in have shot Johnson dead? Could she have had her wound treated by someone other than a doc? Lots of questions here, Sheriff."

"Thanks, Bottoms," Sheriff Silas said to himself. "Young lady Plumb may deserve a look-see."

Chapter Sixteen

YOUNG LADY PLUMB

The knock on the door was solid. Penny was slow to rise from a nap she had been taking on the living room couch. Sammy was out getting groceries.

"Ms. Plumb, please open the door if you are in there. This is Sheriff Silas Slack. I have a few questions to ask you about Bernard Bottoms' death."

Alarm bells went off in Penny's head, but she unlocked the door and invited the beefy sheriff in, offering him a seat on the couch where she had been resting. She couldn't flush the image of him in Bottoms' files with the naked lady from her mind. It was definitely him.

"How can I help you, Sheriff?"

"When was the last time you saw your editor, Ms. Plumb?"

"It's Plum, without the 'b' sound at the end, Sheriff, and I don't recall. I turned in a story on a new small business opening, a diner as I recall, the morning of his demise. I think I saw him briefly then, and everything seemed OK."

"Sorry, Ms. Plum. You didn't see him the afternoon he passed?"

"Not that I can recall, Sheriff. What got him, anyway? Heart attack? Stroke? He seemed to be in good shape. Not a smoker that I knew of. Not overweight," Penny almost added "like you" but stuffed the words.

"Not sure, Ms. Plum. Not exactly sure, which is why I am questioning you."

"You don't suspect foul play, do you, Sheriff?"

"Not sure, Ms. Plum, not exactly sure."

Sammy panicked when he saw the sheriff's car parked in front of their apartment. He didn't know exactly what to do but doubted that this was a positive development. He unlocked the front door and walked in with two bags full of groceries.

"This must be Sammy Spode," said Sheriff Silas. "Can I help you, son," he added, lumbering out of the couch and toward the kitchen.

"No thanks, Sheriff," Sammy said, extending a hand to shake. "Be with you as soon as I get the frozen stuff put up. What's the deal, Sheriff?"

"Just a few questions about Penny's now deceased boss, Bernard Bottoms. Trying to figure out what happened and why. Is it okay if I call you Penny, Ms. Plum?"

"You can call me anything, Sheriff, except Plumb, with a 'b' on the end of it. Bottoms did that all the time, and it irritated the hell out of me."

Sheriff Silas searched her face for any hint of malfeasance but saw none. "Bottoms indicated that you had recently injured your arm, Penny. Can you tell me about it?"

"What does my arm have to do with anything, Sheriff?"

"Just curious and hoping you are better."

"I'm fine, Sheriff."

"Could you show it to me, Penny? Bottoms worried about it and mentioned it to me several times. Would just like a quick look-see."

Penny looked at Sammy, who indicated "no" with a shake of his head.

"Sheriff, I don't have a clue where you are going with this. It has nothing to do with Mr. Bottoms' demise and really is none of your business that I can ascertain. Besides, it is tightly bandaged and healing nicely, and I have no intention of disrupting that process."

"Tightly bandaged by whom, Penny? That's what Bottoms was worried about, that you weren't getting proper care for it. So, you've been treated by a professional?"

"Yes."

"May I ask who?"

Again, Sammy shook his head. Sheriff saw this one.

"What's wrong, Sammy? Just want to make sure your girl-friend is getting proper treatment for her injury."

"A friend," Penny finally answered. "A good friend."

"OK, you two. Thanks for your time and cooperation. Will let you know if I find out anymore about Bottoms' passing. He seemed to have a certain affection for you, Penny, in a fatherly sort of way. We'll stay in touch." Sheriff shook hands with both before exiting.

"Dirty old man. Dirty old men, both of them. Affection, my ass," spat Sammy as he slammed the front door shut.

"Sheriff is on to us, Sammy. I can just feel it. Bottoms told him about my arm and probably my visit to Maude Johnson. Including the fake name. Does he have any rights as a sheriff to come back and demand to see my arm? The bullet's entry and exit points are probably still pretty discernible. Maybe even a scar?"

"Don't know if a search warrant applies to body parts, Penny. Maybe it's time to talk to a lawyer. Someone we can trust."

Chapter Seventeen

A THESIS

Sheriff Silas Slack returned to his office. He was on to something, and he knew it. He needed to learn more about this Penny Plum as soon as possible. Sheriff Googled her name and up she popped, listed among other things, as the author of a history master's degree thesis focused on corporate agriculture. He was able to access the document through her website and began to scroll through it. This was exactly what he suspected and needed to know. He began to jot down notes, trying to summarize her thoughts and conclusions in his own words.

The essence of Penny Plum's provocative piece was that it all happened so quietly and quickly. In fact, most didn't even know what was going down. The multinational corporate takeover of American agriculture, that is.

She staged her thesis with a background summary of the historical importance of family farms in America. From the beginning, a man and a woman would feed themselves and their children from what they produced. Milk from a dairy cow; eggs and fried chicken from their flock of cluckers; tomatoes, beans, and turnips from the garden; chops and loin from a small herd of hogs; water from the well. No row crops, except maybe corn to eat and share with livestock. And, of course, strawberries, which thrived in the thin scrabble soil. No demand for cheap forced labor, as in the Deep South. It was a hardworking but simple lifestyle, wholesome, shared first with neighbors then villagers. Interdependence, collective security. At least a century of tradition and gradual inclusion in small towns that sprung up and flourished.

Penny then proceed to document with academic precision the national transition from family to corporate farming over a few decades.

In the early 1970s Richard Nixon's Assistant Secretary of Agriculture, one Earl Butz, proudly proclaimed that America would put its ingenuity and bounteous natural resources to work "feeding the world." And that we would make good money doing so. "Get big or get out" was his mantra.

Iowa, Nebraska, Kansas, Arkansas, and Illinois became the breadbasket of humanity with gentle climate, plentiful land and water, and vast swaths of fertile soil. Wheat, corn, soybeans. Pork, poultry, beef cattle. A system of mutual interdependence that fed on and fueled each other. Pigs ate the corn, and farmers applied their waste as fertilizer to the beans. And on and on and so on.

Vertical integration, wherein fast-growing corporations obtained control of the levers and components of meat production, eventually morphed horizontally through acquisitions, mergers, and subcontracting. And the closer the farmer could squeeze the porkers and the cluckers together, the more efficient the production lines became. Add some antibiotics to keep intraherd infections at bay and government subsidies to protect against wide product price fluctuations and a closed loop oligarchic system was born.

Demand for fertile land exceeded supply and kicked up the price of entry. As a couple of major international recessions priced credit out of reach of many, small farm foreclosures continued to corporately concentrate the industry, gorging the new economic development model. Consolidation of row crop and meat production brought stability and efficiency to the global table. Multinational agricultural conglomerates propped up smaller proprietors with supplies of live animals to raise, feed to fatten, antibiotics to protect, packing houses to process, and a ready market to sell into. CAFOs exploded across the traditional farming landscape amidst a return to sharecropping, concentrated wealth and power, and subsidized survival.

The new system found permanence, with industry associations showering money on state legislators with demands to reduce regulation and oversight in the name of economic development. Pig bureaus, cattlemen, pork producers, and soybean associations and their well-paid lobbyists set the table. Elected representatives dined lavishly, and voters shrugged "yes."

But beneath it all the water began to sour from the proliferation of animal waste. Aquifers began to shrink as groundwater discharged at a faster rate than it replenished, particularly in the Ogallala mother lode of the Midwest. Surface waters took on a green sheen borne of excess nitrogen and phosphorus runoff. Some drinking water even developed an unpleasant bouquet. And when one state began to grapple with the side effects of corporate farming, another seemed to step up and buy in.

Penny Plum then proceeded to drill down to her homeland.

The state of Missouri began to jump on the corporate ag bandwagon in the early part of the 21st century. It began in earnest with the state legislature restricting an individual's rights to sue agricultural corporations for personal and property damages incurred by their operations and accelerated with the waiver of restrictions on foreign ownership of local farmland to facilitate the purchase of a large domestic meat producer, Smithfield Foods, by a Chinese mega-conglomerate.

Next up was the passage of a "Right to Farm" amendment to the state constitution. Billed as a constitutional protection for family farmers, it was in fact a license to proliferate for large corporate agriculture and hastened the demise of many small farms.

It was followed by successive dilutions in state regulation of CAFOs, including elimination of requirements for construction permits and proof of financial viability by applicants. And the final blow, elimination of the requirement that the Missouri Clean Water Commission, which issues all CAFO permits, must have a majority of independent, not industry, representation on it seven-person board. It was promptly stocked with ag-friendly interests as replacements for independent commissioners. "Members of the public lack the expertise to make good decisions regarding the effects of industry on the state's waterways" was how one of the bill's sponsors put it.

Penny recalled how this comment particularly galled her grandfather, who was one of those independent voices run off the commission. The fact that he had voted against two CAFO permit applications that imperiled small communities and their water supplies merely hastened his departure.

And one final indignity that removed the last line of defense for communities who didn't want the corporate stench as neighbors was the state legislature's unilateral elimination of county health ordinances, which had provided a buffer for more than twenty counties for years. Eliminating local health ordinances and controls pushed Missouri down the same path Iowa had walked in doing so two decades earlier, swelling CAFO numbers from the hundreds to 10,000, and impairing 700 waterways.

The big barn door of deregulation had swung open, never to close again. End of Penny's thesis.

Sheriff Silas was exhausted when he finished. He had not worked his brain this hard since officer training for the St. Louis County Sheriff's Office. And once he had started he couldn't stop. He had plowed through Penny Plum's graduate school thesis in one sitting and had opened the window to a prime murder suspect.

Sheriff cringed at some of Plum's "exaggerations" but marveled at how accurate her overall analysis had been, even back then. Things had generally played out as she described or predicted. He was just happy to be on the winning team and grateful for his relative wealth, frequent "fringe" benefits, and absolute power.

Sheriff was also surprised at how deep Plum's roots ran in the Ozarks. What was it she had written? Eight or nine generations? He would have to be careful how they handled that.

He quickly dialed up the good Deacon Duncan.

"Deak, I've stumbled on to something that I think will be of great interest to you."

Chapter Eighteen

HELP

"**R**ichard, this is Sammy. Need to talk to you."

"Come on out. How's Penny's arm? Bring her along, so I can take a look."

"OK. Be there in an hour."

The first thing Richard did was look after Penny's wound. He was pleased with her recovery, albeit slow, noting that she would always bear scars, both front and back of arm.

"That's why we are here, Richard," Sammy spurted out before catching him up on Editor Bottoms' death, his suspicions about Penny, Penny's confirmation from Maude that Jimmy Johnson's death was not an accident but a shooting, and a strange visit from the county sheriff, who had wanted to see Penny's arm.

Richard was wide-eyed. "You didn't show him, did you, Penny?"

"No, but I have this feeling he will be back. I have no idea if he can make me. It's my body, and I would hope I have some rights to privacy."

"That's why we are here, Richard. Is there a way we can determine if the Posse includes an attorney on its membership roster? I think we are to the point where we need to understand our legal rights in case the sheriff begins to lean on us. And there is one other thing, Richard. It's major. We took a stack of files from Editor Bottoms' office that reveals a vast international conspiracy by three sovereign countries and agents of four corporate agriculture behemoths to control governments and legislatures around the world in pursuit of their self-enriching agenda."

"'The Coalition for Prosperity' they call themselves," Penny added, "and their global mission is deeper and more sinister than your little local Posse could ever have imagined. It has led to the destruction of our local water-based environment and economy, as I'm sure it has to others elsewhere."

Richard sat in shock. "Holy shit" was all he could mutter over and over again.

—ɯ—

"You may be onto something, Sheriff. But we need to be careful, very careful. Has your search of Bottoms' office turned up anything of concern?"

"I'm not totally done yet. There is so much there that I haven't been able to finish it, particularly with the distraction of looking into Bottoms' speculations about Plum. I have found nothing controversial so far, except a couple of file folders with photos of several of our local 'celebrities' in compromising positions with ...you know."

"Any of yours truly?"

"Nope, and the ones I found have been burned to ashes."

"No files about the organization, chain of command, contacts here and around the world? I find that a bit odd, maybe even concerning. Bottoms was purportedly the regional record keeper, the controller of knowledge, the repository of institutional alliances and interactions. Nothing like that at all?"

"No, but then again I haven't finished my inspection."

"I think you need to lock down Bottoms' office and files before you take on this Plum girl as a suspect in Johnson's murder. We have got to control any evidence of collusion and manipulation on the local, national, and international scene, if indeed it exists. I'm not sure I've even seen the whole scheme laid bare. Not sure I want to. Anyway, close that window of potential liability until the assistant secretary's office can get us a new editor. There will always be time to pursue Plum and her boy toy."

"I just know I can nail her, Deak, if I can only get a look at her arm injury. I believe Jimmy Johnson shot her as she was shooting his pigs and before she or Spode killed him. If my instincts are correct, there will be a bullet hole, maybe even an entry and exit mark, to tie her to the crime. Incidentally, can I mandate a strip search?"

"No idea, Silas. But you better be damn careful before you go there. That is what the city attorney is for. You don't want any relevant evidence thrown out because you overstepped. Clean up the damn editor's office, get rid of anything that even reeks of culpability, talk to Bates down at city hall, and then let's get back to organize an appropriate strategy for dealing with Plum. She can wait."

"Yes, sir, Deak."

"So, let me get this straight, Penny and Sammy. You have shot and killed a man, an influential CAFO owner and community leader. Penny has been wounded in the process. Penny has called on the widow using an alias and learned by accident of the murder."

"Please don't use that word, Richard. I didn't mean to. It was self-defense."

"OK, but Penny is now a prime suspect in this 'self-defense.' And in the meantime, you have broken and entered and illegally obtained private documents detailing a deep international agricultural state conspiracy and implicating local civic leaders in a network of bribery and extortion. And local law enforcement is snooping around the corners of your life. And, you say you need an attorney? Sounds to me like you need the attorney general of the United States."

"No way, Richard. He is probably in cahoots with the U.S. assistant secretary of agriculture in all this. We just need someone on our side who we can believe in, who can explain our legal rights to us, and who might have advice as to whom we can trust with our trove of conspiracy documents. Is there anyone in the Posse like that?"

"I don't know, folks, I honestly don't know. In fact I don't know if I even believe you. This is too preposterous, too bizarre, too far-reaching for my little mind to comprehend."

Chapter Nineteen

THE FREE PEOPLE

The Free People, which is what they call themselves, have gathered in a far corner of the Mark Twain National Forest to confab. There were at least 250 of them in all, young and old, male and female. They lived scattered in small family groups or pods throughout the southwestern part of that remote preserve. They gathered during the fall and spring equinox every year to share stories, love, support for their unusual lifestyle, and to find strength in one another.

The moderator blew gently on her flute to gather the group together. It was a lilting, repetitive tune, comforting and commanding at the same time. She stood straight and tall, graying hair at the temples, clad only in a plain sarong but clearly in charge. She answered to Maya.

"Speak to us, Maya," several intoned.

"We are the Free People, gathered here of our own free will, free to do and say what we wish, free to love who we want, free to worship nature in all of her finery and harshness, to protect her from predators who would abuse and destroy her waters, her forests, her grasslands, her earthy bouquet, her intertwining interests with our own. Free to rise up in her defense. This is our manifesto, our creed, our promise to her and to each other."

Most encircling Maya nodded and smiled, some leaked tears, others hugged. Some openly nursed infants. Some slept sitting upright.

"We gather this fall equinox, as we do each spring and fall, to celebrate our freedom, to recommit to preserving it in the face of endless challenges, and to reaffirm our moral commitment to one another."

As Maya continued, others wandered in from their tents in the surrounding woods. Some moved to assist those tending cooking fires on which deer haunches and wild turkey breasts roasted alongside ears of corn and a variety of squashes.

"We will breaking into small groups after dinner to discuss the challenges our members are experiencing and how we might peaceably, when possible, yet resolutely respond. I have gotten word from our cooks that food is now ready for our consumption. I pray a blessing on it and on us in whatever faith tradition, if any, each of us abides."

—⁓—

The Free People come from all walks of life. Many are casualties of the corporate ag takeover of the Ozarks, having lost their family farms or small businesses that depended on the same. Second, third, fourth generations cast aside. As several families sought refuge in the natural fringes that had served them so well in past years, others joined them, and the word spread about alternative means of living and surviving in a world gone mad.

They share common values. A love of the land and the waters of the Ozarks. A work ethic. A devotion to family and friends. A sense of community. A compulsion to adhere to these values and pass them on, believing that they will long outlast the boom-bust mentality of the usurpers.

Farming skills have proved crucial to their shared survival. As do those of craftsmen and carpenters and the few medical practitioners who have joined them. A frontier mentality perpetuates their existence. Codependency strengthens their bonds.

They have their guns, their cell phones, and their battery chargers, and most grow their own weed.

They are a peaceful but hardy lot, capable of taking care of themselves and each other. They exist in another world, beyond the reach of those who would ridicule or hurt them.

A select few of the Free People hide another side, having created a vigilante group. The Posse, they call it. Maya serves as lead deputy, unbeknownst to the majority of those who execute her messaging throughout the Ozarks. Those are mostly common folk, still engaged in mainstream society, but committed to taking back their homeland from the interlopers and profiteers who have desecrated it in the name of money and power. They are a loosely knit select group of individual operators, recruited online by a handful of trusted field operatives with like beliefs, linked only by the ping of periodic text messages that send them forth in the middle of the night to assassinate a dozen pitiful confined animals each, per assigned CAFO site. A frequent and consistent message of resistance to the powers that have become the scourge of the Ozarks.

Though the violence accorded their animal brethren runs counter to their philosophical underpinnings of peace and goodwill, they justify it on the age-old basis of animal sacrifice for the greater good and as a humane alternative to a short lifetime of cramped, feces-laden confinement. They also do so in the hope of revolutionary outcomes one day.

Secrecy is paramount to the survival of the Free People as a tribe, as a lifestyle, and as a resistance. No one must ever connect them to the CAFO incursions or other acts of rebellion, lest they lose their anonymity and be sought out and destroyed.

Chapter Twenty

MISSING

"**S**heriff Slack, this is Av Archibald, the assistant secretary's appointed replacement for the deceased Editor Bottoms, and it is imperative that I speak to you as soon as possible. Could you please come to my office immediately? This is a matter of the utmost urgency."

"I'll be right there."

—⁓—

"Nice to meet you," said Sheriff Silas, extending his hand. "What was the name again?"

"Av Archibald."

"Av? Interesting name. Must be short for something else?"

"Not important, Sheriff Slack. But this is. I understand that you have taken responsibility for securing Bottoms' office and its contents."

"That is correct. And, incidentally, how did you get through the lockdown perimeter I established?"

"Your secretary let me in after I presented my official credentials. She objected initially, but when I pointed out that I was now her boss and she needed to do what I wanted, she concurred with my request. Please don't hold it against her. The point is that I needed to take control of certain sensitive materiel in Bottoms' possession, none of which I can locate. Sheriff, did you remove any papers or files from this office as part of your securitization? Anything?

"It depends, Mr. Archibald. What exactly are you looking for?"

"Just answer the question, Sheriff."

"I guess that I should review your credentials first, Mr. Archibald, or you might write me up."

"OK, Sheriff, I would have had to. Here," Archibald offered, handing an official-looking paper to Sheriff Silas. It bore the seal of the U.S Department of Agriculture and the phrase "Editor, *Spring Town Gazette*" on the "Assignment" line, with an indicated date of "Immediate." Sheriff chuckled when he saw the answer to his first question typed above the "Name" line.

"Avarice, huh? Interesting name, Mr. Archibald. I see why you prefer Av. Who named you and why?

"That is not important, Sheriff, and you may call me Av. Now back to my question. Have you removed anything from Bottoms' office? I received an inventory of what sensitive materials should be in the file door behind his desk. I can find none of them. Have you taken anything?"

"No. Not really."

"Not really, Sheriff?"

"OK, just a couple of 8 x 10 photos of several local officials in, shall we say, sensitive situations. I burned them to prevent undo embarrassment."

"Those were on my inventory list, except there were more than a couple, including several of you, Sheriff."

"Hmmm ...someone must have gotten those, Av."

"They must have gotten a whole lot more, Sheriff. None of what I am looking for is anywhere to be found."

"What would that be, Av?"

"Well, it's top secret information, Sheriff, which means I can't tell you. Has anyone been in Bottoms' office since he died, other than you, Sheriff?"

"Well, let's see. I learned about Bottoms' demise from my deputy, who had received a call from someone. By the time we got to Bottoms' office, the local doctor, and Deacon Duncan, of the pig bureau, were there, praying for the deceased editor as I recall. I assumed control of the office and its contents after they left, and to my knowledge, no one else has entered since then. Except you, utilizing the assistant secretary's key to unlock the door, I presume."

"Correct, Sheriff. Just how many keys to the office are there, Sheriff? And who discovered the body. Who called your deputy to report the death? And was the secretary under strict orders to allow no one to enter? Did you dust for fingerprints in the office? And—"

"Hold on, Av, you're going too fast. One question at a time, please. Yes, until you strong-armed the secretary, no one was allowed in. And it is my understanding that there are three keys to the office. The one I've been using. The one you used. And the one I put in the desk middle drawer."

"I did not look for fingerprints as it was clear that Bottoms had died of natural causes, and there was no need to treat his office as a crime scene."

"And yet you secured the office, Sheriff?"

"At Deacon Duncan's request, Av. He had this vague notion, consistent with your more documented one, about sensitive records and documents in Bottoms' possession, probably in his office. He wanted me to scrub the office clean and secure them if found."

"And you found nothing, Sheriff?"

"Nothing, if you consider a photo of the mayor with a naked floozy on his lap nothing. Nothing, if two city council members were photographed in a hot tub with eight unclothed women. Nothing if—"

"Enough, Sheriff. No philosophical manifests? No documents? No contact names and phone numbers? No bank records? Nothing of a potentially incriminating nature?"

"No, Av, nothing like that."

"OK, Sheriff, let's go back to discovery of the body and reporting to authorities."

"I presume the secretary called my deputy and that she was the one who discovered the body."

"Do you know if the office door was locked then and she used her key to enter?"

"Well, let's ask her, Av."

"Why didn't you, Sheriff? Isn't it normal to ask such questions, Sheriff?"

"Yes, if a crime is suspected. A man dead of a heart attack with a sobbing secretary sharing the news didn't strike me as a crime scene, Av. Do you expect foul play? Could Bottoms have been murdered, Av?"

"Not likely, Sheriff. But if sensitive or confidential documents have been absconded with, yes. If those documents could be used to bring harm to U.S. government authorities, yes. That's foul play."

"What are you looking for, Av?"

"As indicated previously, Sheriff Slack, I can't tell you. I will need to visit with you and Mr. Deacon Duncan soon, but first I need to contact the assistant secretary's office."

Chapter Twenty-One

CONTACTS

Hi, Sammy, Richard here. I'm sorry."

"What?"

"I'm sorry, Sammy. I apologize for my overreactions to your and Penny's dilemma. You just really caught me by surprise. And I am worried about the two of you. I've given serious thought to your question about who in the Posse might be able to help you with legal advice and even interpreting and safeguarding the documents you have obtained. I have some ideas to share. Is it okay if I stop by this evening?"

"You bet, Richard."

—⁓—

Prior to contacting Sammy, Richard had taken a major risk. He sat down with his cell phone and backpedaled to the last "mission" message he had received, which ironically was the night that Sammy and Penny had gotten into this mess. He knew that his original instructions warned that no attempt should be ever be made to respond to texts from the number, that any attempt to do so would be ignored, and that disciplinary action could include disbarment from the Posse. Yet he felt he had no choice. So, he typed it out, a personal plea.

"OK, whoever you are. This is Posse member Dr. Richard Bloom, and I desperately need to talk to someone. A fellow Posse member is in deep trouble, and in possession of potentially damaging information on the bad guys. He needs advice and protection. Please respond with contact information."

Several minutes later Richard's phone pinged. The short message read "Call me at 417-334-3398 in exactly one hour."

A female voice answered the phone. "Is this Dr. Richard Bloom?"

"Yes."

"Prove it."

"My wife is Lucinda, I call her Lucy, and we live at 524 Powell Drive. I am a veterinarian, and have two dogs of my own, Masters and Thesis—"

"That's enough, Dr. Bloom. How can I help you or your fellow Posse member who seems to have gotten in trouble?"

"Sammy Spode needs to speak to an attorney or someone he can trust as soon as possible."

"I am both of those. You mentioned murder and incriminating documents in the same breath. Can you tell me more?"

"Only what they have shared with me," Richard responded. He proceeded to describe the first visit by Sammy and his girlfriend Penny and the treating of her gunshot wound.

"We know all of that, Richard. Remember the message you got to bench Sammy indefinitely? We are aware of what happened, of the murder, of his stupid inclusion of a girlfriend in a field exercise. What about the documents, Richard? Have you seen them?"

"No, but Sammy said they present a vast international conspiracy, controlled by several nations and corporate agriculture behemoths, set on self-enrichment and evasion of all norms, controls, and regulations. A Coalition of—or for—Prosperity or something like that."

"Hmmmm … tell me more, Richard."

"That is all I know …by the way, what is your name?"

"Not important. I have Spode's phone number. Tell him I will call at precisely 9:00 his time tonight. He is to have no other person in the room beyond this Penny and you, if you choose to stay involved. No one, absolutely no one, must know of this call."

—◊—

"OK, gentlemen. We have a problem, a big problem, and you are going to help me remedy it."

Sheriff Silas Slack and Deacon Duncan sat across from Avarice Archibald in the new editor's office at the *Spring Town Gazette*. He twirled his chair around to face the file cabinets behind him and waved his hand the length of the row.

"I have been through each drawer and each file in Bottoms' file cabinets and his desk as well and can't find them."

"What is 'them?'" asked Deak.

"I am cleared by the assistant secretary himself to tell you, but if you share this information with anyone else, it will be a death penalty."

Sheriff Silas looked at Deak in confusion. "Not sure I want to know under those circumstances," he whispered meekly.

"Well, neither of you has any choice at this point," answered Av. "The front door is locked, the door to this office is locked, and you are not leaving until we reach an understanding about the magnitude of our shared problem and a plan to address it. Sheriff, you have previously stated that you have removed nothing from Bottoms' entire office except a couple of incriminating photos. Do you swear this is true?"

"Well, I did help carry his stiff carcass out."

"Do you swear, Sheriff?"

"Yes, I swear, Av."

"And you, Duncan, you have removed nothing from this office either? Do you swear?"

"Yes, I swear."

"OK, gentlemen, let me explain what is missing and why it is critical that we recover it, lest it fall into unfriendly hands."

The phone in Sammy and Penny's apartment rang at exactly 9p.m., as promised. Sammy picked it up and said, "Sammy Spode, here."

"OK, Spode. Who is with you and why? I mean everyone in the room or within earshot of this conversation. Please put your phone on speaker and let them introduce themselves."

Sammy punched the speaker icon. Penny went first.

"This is Penny Plum. I am Sammy's fiancée"—Sammy jumped to attention. This was the first time Penny had ever used the "F," as in fiancée, word. His heart felt like it would explode as he tried to control his emotions—"and I am the one who was wounded; the one who is a suspect in a murder investigation; the one who worked for the editor at the local epicenter of an international agribusiness conspiracy; the one who found the editor dead of a heart attack and stole incriminating documents, photos, and bank records from his office; and the one who is frankly scared to death."

"You've been a busy young lady these past few weeks, haven't you?"

"And who are you, if I may?"

"You may, all you wish, but my name is not important. The fact that I am an attorney and a trusted member of the Posse leadership is. And despite your uninvited intrusion into our group, you can trust me, too, Penny. Who else is in the room? Please identify yourselves."

"This is Dr. Richard Bloom, fellow Posse member with Sammy, and the one who reached out to you. Thank you for responding."

"And me, Sammy. That's it. Just the three of us."

"Let's start with you, Penny. Why do you think they suspect you in the murder of Jimmy Johnson?"

"First and foremost, the wound. Dr. Bloom treated me efficiently and effectively the night of the shooting, and I will always be grateful," Penny shared, with a nod of her head toward Richard. "But he had to bandage it, put it in a sling, treat a follow-up infection in it, and generally lay it out there for my whole world, including Editor Bottoms, to notice. And I was probably too evasive initially in responding to Bottoms' questioning. I think it aroused suspicions in him. And then I made the mistake of visiting the widow of Jimmy Johnson, who accidentally revealed that his murder was being covered up."

"Again, Penny. Please don't use that word. It was self-defense, not murder," pled Sammy.

"Sorry, Sammy, but that's how they view it. Anyway, I used an alias with Maude Johnson, who immediately reported it to Bottoms, thanking him for sending me by with the newspaper's condolences. Since he hadn't actually done so, and that was my cover for going, he began to question me with regularity and did so until he died. I didn't realize that he had reported his suspicions to Sheriff Slack until I found a note in Bottoms' office. Slack's visit two days ago, almost demanding to see my wound, set off the alarm bells that led us back to Richard and now to you. I know he knows that he will find evidence of a bullet wound if he ever gets a look. And that is question number one. Can he force me to show him?

"Yes, Penny. He can."

Chapter Twenty-Two

THE CIRCLE TIGHTENS

Deacon Duncan and Sheriff Silas sat listening in stunned silence as Avarice Archibald laid out the list of items that should have been in Editor Bottoms' secured files. The gravity of his disclosures hit home immediately. Both knew, as "local coordinators," that they were part of something larger and probably more sinister, but neither had any idea of how much so.

Archibald laid out his theory that someone had found Bottoms just after he died while his office and the files he was working on were exposed. That he or she or they chose not to call for help but to rifle through his file cabinet and desk, removing the most sensitive folders, including ones marked "Top Secret," and had possession of them right now—if they hadn't already been turned over to authorities or the press, which seemed unlikely since no news had broken.

"Our job is to locate the thieves and their bounty, eliminate all of the above, and restore A Coalition for Prosperity to its rightful position of dominance in the world."

"I think I know where to begin, Av," stated Sheriff Silas. "But I will first have to obtain legal authority to serve a Ms. Penny Plumb with a search warrant that includes the right to conduct a strip search."

—◊—

"How can that be, Ms. Whatever-Your-Name-Is? What right does anyone have to remove my clothing and view my body?"

"Have you ever heard the term 'strip search,' Penny?"

"Yes, but I thought that was used to look for drugs in anuses or weapons and the like?"

"It generally is, Penny. The Fourth Amendment to the Constitution protects against unreasonable searches and seizures. But the state of Missouri has its own take. While authorities generally can't strip-search for non-felonies in the state, an exception allows it when there is probable cause of finding evidence of commission of a crime. Your bullet hole provides such evidence."

"Do you mean that f-ing sheriff can walk into my apartment and rip off my top in search of a bullet hole?"

"No, he would need a search warrant, a female assistant to conduct the search, and a place where your privacy can be assured. All of which he can readily obtain and may be in the process of doing so as we speak."

"Yes, Sheriff Slack. I can issue a search warrant, which will include the option for a strip search if you deem it relevant to uncovering evidence of commission of a crime. But you will need a female deputy to conduct the search in complete privacy."

"We don't have any of those, counselor, female detectives, that is."

"Well, you had better get one on board quickly if I am to authorize this particular search warrant."

After consultation with Deak and Av, Sheriff Silas deputized his secretary, Stephanie Char, and informed her that she would need to conduct a strip search of a suspect immediately.

"What do I do, Sheriff Silas?"

"I don't know? I guess you take her into a bedroom and ask her to remove her clothes. In this case her top will do as we are only interested in looking at a wound on her arm, which will likely be heavily bandaged, and determining if it is a bullet hole."

"What if she won't disrobe, and how do I know if it looks like a bullet hole?"

"I don't know. Pull her top off? Rip off the bandage? Take a picture with your cell phone? You're a lot bigger than she is, do whatever you need to. This is a potential murderer, Ms. Char, and you need to help us close the loop. I don't think she is dangerous, but who knows if she is desperate. Be careful, Ms. Char, but be strong. I will be the room next door if things get out of hand, and I've got you covered."

"When do we do this, conduct this strip search thing?"

"I'm thinking catch them off guard, maybe tomorrow about suppertime."

"But Fred will want me fixing supper for him like I always do."

"Who is Fred?"

"He is my live-in, and he can be pretty demanding."

"Well, tell Fred that you will return with a $100 bill to take him to dinner anywhere he wishes after we've busted this murderer or her accomplice. Meet you here at the office tomorrow at 5:50?"

"Yes, sir, Sheriff Silas, yes, sir."

—⁂—

"So, what do we do next?"

"Well, Penny, first things first. We have to get you out of harm's way immediately.

"What does that mean, ma'am?"

"I know a place that we can hide you and Sammy away, indefinitely if need be. It will be pretty rustic, make that primitive, but you will be safe there. What do you think about the great outdoors, woods, creeks, one bath a week, a fireplace for warmth as we move into winter? Essentially, roughing it?

"We like all of that, to visit, not to spend the rest of our lives in."

"Have you ever heard of the Free People, Penny?"

"No, but this vision of living in a rural ghetto for the rest of my life keeps popping into my mind."

"The Free People consider it more of a rural paradise, where they can live, be, do anything they want. They intentionally escape from the corruption and hatred that our world has become, beyond the fouled waters and putrid air, the crime and the poverty, the haves and have nots."

"Now, you are making more sense. Where can such a place exist in the Ozarks today? All I see is ruin and decay, sadness, and slobbering up to the current powers that have become the dominant class, the ones who have usurped the rights of rightful heirs to the waters, the forests, the very air we breathe. Where can this be, ma'am?"

"Have you ever heard of Goose Creek, Penny?"

"Only eight or ten generations of tall tales."

"Good. The upper reaches of the Goose Creek watershed have been shielded from desecration by the Mark Twain National Forest and nurtured by the caring hearts of the Free People."

"That's just what you said, Sammy, without the people part."

"There are other safe havens spread around the edges, but this one is close, and I know a family that would welcome you into their midst. Jai and Karma have just added onto their small cabin in anticipation of the arrival of their first child next spring."

"You mean we can just barge in on a young couple soon to be with child and they would accept us?

"Yes, except they are not young, Penny. Jai is in his sixties and Karma at least forty, and both left behind abusive relationships and toxic environments to begin anew in the wilderness."

"How do you know all of this? That they would take us in? That they would want unknown company in this personal time of new beginnings, including a child?"

"Because that is the way of the Free People. That is all I need to know, and you will come to know. Anyway, we have got to get you out of here before the sheriff returns with a search warrant. I want you to pack one suitcase each of clothing and personal items you will need to get through winter with Jai and Karma. You will leave everything else behind, and we will pay your monthly rent ahead to protect what you leave."

"Do Jai and Karma have a last name?"

"No, they left those behind too. And there is one more thing. The files. We have to protect our possession of those files until someone can fully analyze and translate into action. How big is the whole cache?"

"The biggest one, and probably most important, is the vision thing for A Coalition for Prosperity. It is thick and filled with conceptual justification. It is a most incriminating piece of evidence of a multinational scheme to, in essence, take over the world through agriculture. At least as best as I can tell. I have read it twice and as an investigative reporter remain overwhelmed. The rest of the files are for the most part 'on-the-ground' tactical machinations and hard evidence of bribery and corruption. Just say that Sammy and I were able to carry the whole mess ourselves on one trip."

"OK, you need to make one more trip with the whole mess. First thing tomorrow morning you need to put everything in a backpack or a carry-on case or something that hides the contents and go the Spring Town Community Bank. You will ask for the president, Jarrod Combs. He is a friend of ours. I will give him a heads up that you will be needing at least a couple of safe deposit boxes to store some family history in. You will also need two keys to however many boxes it takes. He won't ask any questions."

"Is he a member of the Posse?" asked Richard, who had been quiet the whole conversation, again not quite believing what he was hearing.

"I can't tell you. Just like I can't tell him if you might be. Anyway, be there before 8 a.m., and he will handle the rest. Penny and Sammy, you will keep one key to each of the boxes. You will give the others to Richard to keep for me until I can arrange for their delivery. Are you okay with that, Richard? It could be dangerous if these papers are as explosive as Penny and Sammy say?"

"Yes."

"Penny and Sammy, you will keep your set of keys on your person at all times, maybe for the rest of your lives. I do not want you accessing the box until cleared personally by me."

"So, let me get this straight, Ms. Whomever-You-Are-Besides-A-Lawyer," Penny suddenly burst in. "You want Sammy and me to slip away into a primitive paradise with two middle-aged so-called 'Free People' who are in the throes of a late-in-life pregnancy and have no last name, to be prepared to settle into their rustic dwelling and lifestyle for the foreseeable future, and give up a set of keys and access to the only leverage we have in the world to protect ourselves from evil to someone who won't even share their name with us?"

"Yes, and be prepared to leave under the cover of darkness tomorrow evening. I will have a driver pick you up, and you will leave your vehicles behind. I will text the driver's identity and clearance password to you after I've had time to alert Jai and Karma that you will be coming to live with them. If the sheriff confronts you before we've cleared you out, do not let him or his deputy conduct a full body search under any circumstances. If he pushes, call this number and explain that your attorney will discuss his request with him. I will be on call the next forty-eight hours.

Again, do not let anyone touch you. If he insists, I will have someone outside your apartment to intervene."

Penny looked at Sammy, then Richard, and shook her head back and forth several times. "This is crazy. The whole mess is beyond comprehension. I'm not sure we should do this."

"Do you have a better idea?" asked Sammy softly.

Chapter Twenty-Three

ON THE LAM

It was after midnight, and Penny was overwhelmed. She didn't know who to trust, why, or how. Except Sammy. The lady she had spoken with seemed legitimate, at least in terms of looking out for their lives. But how could they know? And this whole disappearing act into a magical world of alternative reality nagged at her common sense.

She and Sammy shared their doubts, their fears, and their lack of options as they stuffed winter clothing into their respective suitcases. Their conversation became even more agitated as they began to carefully place the stolen documents in two backpacks.

"These papers are the only things in the world that can save us if we are ever apprehended, Sammy. And we are giving up total control of them to a mystery lady lawyer without a name, a banker we don't know, and your friend Richard who seems no more than a pawn in a monster game."

"I trust them, Penny. For some reason my instincts flash green lights."

"I don't, Sammy. There are lots of yellow flashes going off in my brain, with a few red ones to boot. Is there any place in this apartment where we could hide something that could never be discovered by another? A nook, or cranny, or dark corner where we would know our secret would be safe, no matter what?"

"Well, there's that ceiling tile in the bathroom that is slightly discolored, the one we have promised to replace but never have. It's a false ceiling as I discovered while messing around up there. Why?"

"I think we need to preserve a copy of a couple of key pages of this stuff, something tangible that we can always come back to. Just in case. I don't trust anybody, Sammy, except you."

"Glad I made the cut, particularly since I'm the one in the most potential trouble."

"I don't think the ceiling tile trick is foolproof, Sammy. How about this? I'll photograph a few pages of the "manifesto," including the cover and visioning pages, on my cell phone? I will send them to my folks in Boston, telling them that it is a new novel I'm working on, that I wanted to share it with them, their eyes only, since the ideas are so wild and crazy, and I don't want anyone stealing them. I'll ask them to just store in their cell phone photo album until I finish and find a publisher. That way it will always be there for me to come back to if I get off track. What do you think, Sammy?"

"Well, this whole affair is stranger than fiction, so it will probably work."

"I can't sleep, Sammy. We're all packed. Want to make love?"

The early morning trip to the bank was traumatic at best. It took two large safe deposit boxes to hold their treasure trove of evidence and smut. Inside the safe deposit box vault they carefully unloaded their backpacks, putting most of the visioning, planning, and organizational materials in one, and the incriminating photos, bank records, and other evidence of malfeasance in the other.

Banker Combs was most cooperative and calming, standing watch outside the vault as they went about their business. They requested and received two sets of keys for each box as instructed.

Penny glanced over her shoulder with what bordered on regret as they left the secure area, knowing that their only certain line of defense was now to be in the hands of an unknown. They dropped a set of keys at Richard's for safekeeping until the mystery lady could pick them up and went home to secure their own. Penny decided that she would wear them on a long gold chain around her neck, tucked safely between her breasts, never to be revealed nor removed. Except to Sammy, of course, as he was quick to point out.

The knock on the door at six that evening caught Penny and Sammy off guard. They had received the ID info and code from their unnamed lawyer, but their driver wasn't due until seven or so. They decided to ignore.

"Ms. Plumb, we know you are in there. Please open or we will have to break down the door. This is Sheriff Silas Slack and my deputy Stephanie Char. We have some important questions to ask and a search warrant if you choose not to cooperate."

Penny looked at Sammy in panic and motioned for him to go the bedroom and hide their suitcases somewhere, anywhere.

"Hold on, Sheriff. We are just getting dressed, and I will open up when we are finished."

Sheriff looked at Deputy Char and mouthed an expletive. "Just getting dressed?" he whispered. "At six o'clock in the evening?"

"Open up now, Ms. Plumb, or I am coming in."

Penny hesitated then cracked the door, with the safety chain still engaged. "The name is Plum, without the 'b,' Sheriff, and what do you want?"

"We want to come in, Plumb, and this here search warrant gives us the right to do so."

"You stay right where you are, Sheriff Slack. I am dialing my attorney to seek counsel about whether I need to accede to this ridiculous invasion of privacy. I am sure you will want visit with her before you cross a line that will get you in trouble."

"So, you need a lawyer now? What in the world for, I might ask, if you have done nothing wrong?"

"To protect me from illegal harassment by a corrupt law enforcement agency, Sheriff."

Ten minutes later with sheriff and attorney now screaming at one another on Penny's phone, gear safely stowed under the bed, and Sammy sitting stiffly on the couch with his deer rifle splayed across his lap, Penny calmly unlatched the door, providing entry to the sheriff and his deputy. Penny invited both inside, leaving the speaker function on her phone on, and asked the sheriff what he could possibly want at this hour of the day. He refused her offer to sit down, continuing to stand just inside the front door.

"I have some questions for you, Ms. Plumb. Were you at work at any time during the day that editor Bernard Bottoms passed away?"

"Should I answer?" Penny asked her phone.

"Sure," was the response.

Penny hoped that meant help was on the way. "Yes, Sheriff, and if you call me Plumb, with a 'b' one more time, I am going to spit in your face."

"You go, girl," Sammy said with a laugh, although he was less confident that there was someone coming to the rescue than in his ability to defend themselves if needed. If he was going to be accused of being a murderer, he might as well earn the distinction. His presence and weapon had not gone unnoticed by Deputy Char, who nodded toward it while nudging the sheriff's arm.

"Was anyone else in the office while you were there that day, Plum?"

"I don't recall, Sheriff. Could have been? I was working on a story due the next afternoon."

"Did you speak to or see Editor Bottoms at any time while you were working?"

"No, he kept his office door closed and locked."

"How do you know it was locked, Plum?"

"Well, it always was, so I assumed this day was no different than any other."

"I think you are lying, Plum, flat-out lying. I believe you were there when Bottoms died, that you entered his office, and—rather than call for help—removed private information from his files, and, in essence, stole it for your own selfish ends."

"Absolutely not, Sheriff. And what kind of information could possibly be so important that you are accusing me of stealing it?"

"I also believe that you shot and killed Jimmy Johnson and were wounded in the exchange of gunfire. That the wound beneath your bandage is that of a bullet hole," the sheriff continued without answering.

This set Sammy to stirring on the couch and fiddling with his rifle and Penny's attorney to protesting in the background.

Sheriff Silas Slack didn't stop. "Plum, I have here a strip search warrant because I believe you are hiding evidence of commission of a crime under that bandage. You have a right to privacy and a female searcher, so I recommend that Deputy Char accompany you back to your bedroom and observe you removing your top and the bandage on your arm."

"I'm sorry, Sheriff, but you have no right to order any violation of my personal privacy by this bimbo or anyone else. I refuse to subject myself to this indignity."

"Guess we will have to arrest you then, Plum."

"On what charges, Sheriff?'

"I don't know, Plum. Resisting arrest? Failure to abide by a search warrant? Insubordination? We'll worry about that when—"

Both Penny and Sammy had seen the front door crack open behind Sheriff Slack and Deputy Char. A shadow emerged from the darkness, raised a blunt object, and struck the sheriff on the head, dropping him like a rock. Deputy Char screamed and ran from the assailant, ripping her badge from her chest and whining that she didn't get paid enough for this. She was soon bound, along with the sheriff, and locked in the sheriff's squad car.

"Grab your bags and let's get out of here," the voice behind the mask commanded. "Glad you are okay and on your way," the voice in the phone yelled. "I love you," Penny whispered to Sammy.

Chapter Twenty-Four

JAI AND KARMA

"**Y**ou are heroes to us," proudly announced Jai as he greeted Penny and Sammy at the front door to his small cabin with a warm embrace. Karma tried but featured too much baby in front to close a hug.

"Heroes?" Penny shrugged in confusion.

"You took on the Man and have lived to tell about it. We don't know all of the details, just that you have been forced into hiding for something to do with standing up to the scourge that has consumed the Ozarks we all know and love. You are welcome in our house for as long as you wish to be here."

Jai was a short, balding, muscular man with a gray bushy beard and engaging smile. Karma was the picture of peace, soft face, big brown eyes, and bulging belly. Their homestead was as described: small, cozy, warmed by a large natural rock fireplace. There were two rooms in addition to the main living, cooking, and eating area. Both were open to the fireplace for warmth and appeared to have rudimentary double beds in them. Penny assumed one was to become the baby's room at some point, so despite Jai's earnestness, the invitation was probably not as open-ended as it seems. A concern for later. Now was now, and here was here.

"As you can see, our home is not fancy, but it has served us well since we moved here two years ago. Please sit down, and let's get to know one another better. Have you eaten supper yet?"

"No, we haven't," answered Penny, "but please don't worry. We are just grateful to be here."

"How does fresh mushroom soup sound, with a crust of bread," asked Karma?

"Divine!"

—⟋ɷ⟍—

The morning dawned sparkling and bright. Penny and Sammy's room had no window, but it didn't take long for light to creep into the cabin and get them stirring.

They had learned the night before, as they conversed into the early hours of the morning, how Jai and Karma had come to be here and now.

Jai had sold real estate in Spring Town and surrounding communities since graduating from technical school, which he had attended after losing his sales job with a local manufacturer when it was acquired by and merged into a foreign-owned company, early in Jai's middle-aged life. That seeming misfortune cost him his sobriety, his first marriage, and his family in the aftermath.

Yet it seemed to have been the best thing that had ever happened to him as he ultimately established a small but successful regional real estate business. That it gradually came to depend more and more on the sale of small family farms and rural businesses to out-of-state entities with murky credentialing and financing initially escaped his scrutiny. Limited liability companies were often the agents of purchase and wired-in funds the purchase of closure. Jai's cut was always delivered in full and on time, no questions asked or allowed. He was known in this life as George, George Jones.

The added distraction of falling head over heels in love with pretty Kay Corona took most of his attention away from what he was witnessing on the ground.

Kay was twenty years his junior, but that didn't dim the magical connection that emerged from their first date, which began with dinner and ended with an overnight in her small apartment. They had met in the checkout line at a supermarket and chatted each other up while waiting, which was really not either of their styles. Kay had just come off of a two-year failed romance on the heels of a disastrous run at marriage and was desperate for kindness and respect. She sensed both in George's demeanor at first brush.

George was so entombed in closing business deals that he rarely noticed something he thought was simply beautiful. Kay was that to him and drew his attention.

They agreed to grab a cup of coffee in the adjoining coffee shop, which led to a dinner invite the following evening. Neither could remember who invited whom in their respective tellings of the encounter to Penny and Sammy, and both laughed playfully at the memory. Both confessed to being enamored of the other immediately.

It was shortly thereafter that an unknown Chinese national approached George with a "business deal" over coffee that made him squirm inside. "Literally squirm," he had emphasized to Penny and Sammy. The small man with the clipped accent had been on the receiving end of several of George's recent deals and complimented him on his knowledge of local real estate values. The man, who used only a first name, Mel, wanted to do more business with George. In fact, he wanted to do a whole lot more business and was willing to put George on a large up-front retainer to find him deals. George had never heard of such an arrangement for a small player like himself but listened closely to the proposition.

Mel would pay George $500,000 in cash, which he currently had stashed in the back of his car if George would focus on finding him farmers around the region who had spurned previous offers of fair pricing for their acreage and might be talked into selling at prices quadruple the market.

When George asked why, Mel informed him that demand for pork was insatiable in his homeland and enormously profitable export contracts were currently available. Mel's traditional efforts at land acquisition had been successful initially, but his government procurement agencies were upping the ante for CAFO-based pork production. He asked if George knew about CAFOs, and George assured him that he had sold land for herd expansion and conversion with increasing frequency. Mel noted that he was authorized to not only offer mega-premium pricing for land but also lucrative long-term employment contracts to sellers who wished to augment their haul by staying on as CAFO managers.

Where was all this money coming from and why, George had wondered to himself as he promised to consider Mel's retainer offer and meet with him in three days to formally respond. Mel would have a contract drawn up and the funds available for George in a large suitcase. This time they would meet in George's modest office.

In the meantime, George took it on himself to drive back to several of the farm properties he had closed on in the past six months. What he found turned his stomach. In all cases small family farms had been converted into confined animal feeding operations with thousands of pigs crammed into containment barns and their waste pooled in adjoining settlement basins. The stench was horrid, the visuals frightening, and the runoff into wetlands or small streams in neighboring areas was clogged with muck and algae.

George could only ask two questions. Were there no regulations regarding CAFOs and their waste in local or state jurisdictions? How could he have been party to such a destructive pattern of industrial farming and not noticed it?

The answer to question one was easily answered with an internet search of the Missouri Department of Natural Resources website. *No* No, there were no significant regulations prohibiting or controlling the development of CAFOs in state government. And *no*. No local ordinances could be more rigid in regulation than those imposed by the state. Protections had been dumbed down to the lowest common denominator. George was appalled. No wonder the Ozarks and its water had gone straight to hell. Just as he hoped the perpetrators of this destruction would follow.

The answer to question two was perhaps even more troubling. He simply had paid no attention to the consequences of his recent business dealings because the money had been good and the clients willing and able to deal quickly and efficiently, the magic elixir for every real estate broker who had ever been.

On night two of his grace period, he had sat down with Kay and shared his disgust with himself and what was happening in Ozarks. He confirmed the money and contractual arrangement he had been offered by whom he presumed was an agent of the Chinese government two days earlier. And he reported on the disasters that had become of several of his recent sales transactions with this previously unknown client.

"George, do you really think this guy is going to show up with a half-million dollars to hand over to you tomorrow in return for you recruiting more victims for his corporate farming scheme?"

"I do." He then wondered aloud if Kay would run away from this mess with him.

"Where, George? And you would really walk away from that kind of money?"

"Yes, if you will come with me, Kay."

Jai confirmed that George Jones was not at his office when Mel, his contract, and his suitcase full of dollars appeared at the appointed time the following afternoon.

Penny and Sammy had sat transfixed by George's/Jai's guilt-laden confession, despite the early morning hour.

"I am so sorry to go on like this," he continued. "But there is more. And then we want to hear all about you two."

Chapter Twenty-Five

NUTS AND BOLTS

Sheriff Silas was in no mood to be interrogated by a pip-squeak new editor from the assistant secretary's office, no matter how important he was.

"Shut up, Avarice Archibald. Yes, I know I should have taken more men with me and not a cowardly woman, but I had no idea that I would meet with physical resistance."

Sheriff Slack and Deputy Char had been discovered bound and gagged just two hours earlier, after having spent a very cold night huddled together in the back of the sheriff's squad car.

"You can berate me all you want, Archibald, but that is not going to get our murderers back or the precious stack of documents you want."

"Easy, Silas," warned Deacon Duncan. "Avarice has been sent to help us, not round us up and convict us of being crooked. How do you know these suspects are the ones or even if they have all the evidence of conspiracy Archibald shared with us as missing?"

"I just know it, Deak. Penny Plumb or Sammy Spode shot and killed Jimmy Johnson as he was trying to protect his hogs and as he wounded Plumb in the process. Somehow they found medical care for Plumb, but the scar that bears the mark of a bullet will never go away. And then Plumb stumbled onto a dead Editor Bottoms at her place of work, with his office unlocked. She, and maybe her sidekick, stole top secret classified U.S. government documents that can get us and a whole lot of people much more important than us thrown into jail, convicted of treason, or even assassinated. Them's the facts as I see them, Deak. We have got to track down Plumb and Spode and whomever it was that cold-cocked me as soon as we can."

"That is all Archibald is saying Silas, and he can bring resources to the table who can help us do it."

"Enough gentlemen, enough. Let's go back to the beginning, Sheriff. I'm going to put Agent Smiley, FBI, on the speaker phone to hear what happened."

"How much does Smiley know about the operation?" mouthed Deak silently to Av.

"Nothing" whispered Av back to him. "And we need to keep it that way."

"You mean to tell me the entire security apparatus of the United States government has been kept out of the loop? That little old Sheriff Slack and Deak Duncan know more than the FBI or CIA?"

"There is a rogue branch of the CIA that has operated under the jurisdiction of the Department of Agriculture that is involved, but nothing beyond that. That is the way the creators planned it, and it applies to other intelligence agencies of partner countries as well."

"How can that be? These spooky guys all over the world know everything?"

"Not about A Coalition for Prosperity. That is the whole point. This is not a state or deep state or even government-sponsored initiative. It has been conceived and is managed outside the traditional corridors of power. Which is why it has been so effective and efficient in delivering wealth and power to its creators and its creators only."

"I don't think I want to know any more," mumbled Deak. The sheriff could only shake his head.

"Well, you need to, Deak. Each country, each corporation, has its own layers of knowledge and authority, the less of each the further down the line. You, the sheriff, and Bottoms were known as regional operatives in our operational structure. You promoted unfettered CAFO development in the Ozarks because we rewarded you with lucrative positions and attractive fringes. It was your job to keep things growing regionally and suppress anything bad that might scare off potential investors. You put buyers and sellers of farmland together and didn't interfere with Chinese or Brazilian freelancers out cutting their own deals. Financing came from offshore untraceable sites, and livestock, feed, medicine, and markets were provided by our corporate partners. They also bought and sold legislators and local politicians, paying them to lessen or eliminate useless regulations in favor of mass production. They controlled markets around the world, and everyone who played the game got a significant skim off of the profits. Oligopolistic Capitalism the academics call it, A Coalition for Prosperity to us.

"Why Spring Town? Because of the Ozarks. Because of the unique water resources, cheap land, and cultural anti-regulation bias. The Ozarks was one of five initial key target markets identified by the assistant secretary of agriculture's office for exploitation. The others bear similar traits but are geographically dispersed to avoid attracting undo attention. Each target market has regional operatives like you three, a direct report in the assistant secretary's office who is privy to most of the grand scheme and compensated well for loyalty and confidentiality and who in turn reports to the assistant secretary himself. And then there is the small support staff, like yours truly, who simply plugs in where and when needed. We all live a pretty good life, I think you will agree.

"Our partner countries and multinational companies are structured similarly with focus on compensation, bribery, and if all else fails, elimination to protect our respective secrets. You now fall into that privileged class, gentlemen. Am I clear?"

"Yes, sir," a wide-eyed Deacon Duncan stammered, as Sheriff Slack nodded in cowed agreement.

"Are we ready for Agent Smiley, gentlemen? Remember always that he is an outsider brought in to assist in your investigation, Sheriff. I, through you, must never lose control of the process. These are my direct orders from the assistant secretary's office. Smiley's involvement is occasioned by the premeditated murder of a local citizen of high repute and the theft of top-secret U.S. government documents by the murderers, documents that he must never see. We might even be able to pin Bottoms' death on the suspects before we are finished."

"Agent Smiley, FBI, meet Sheriff Silas Slack and his community liaison, Deacon Duncan. We appreciate your willingness to assist in our investigation of at least one brutal murder and the theft of secret documents that might prove to be a security risk to our country."

Chapter Twenty-Six

JAI AND KARMA, CONTINUED

"**A**nyway, Kay accepted my offer to leave and start over together, somewhere else, without the money or the guilt of being an accomplice to a murder of sorts. She even had an idea where we might find temporary shelter in case the Chinese guy was severely pissed and tried to chase me down. Please take it from here, Kay."

"OK, hon. I worked for a branch office of a national environmental organization, trying to bring attention to the travesty that was engulfing the Ozarks. As you might expect, we weren't particularly popular among the powers that had assumed control of the city and the county. We received death threats constantly and occasionally vandalism directed toward our small office rather than ourselves. The office was actually a co-op, housing several entities engaged in environmental snooping and reporting, and we clung tightly together for security.

One day a friend asked me if I had ever thought about dropping out of the societal mess we had created in the region. I confessed that I hadn't, but it didn't sound half bad if things continued to spiral down. She claimed to have a close friend who was considering just that but was very secretive as to how and where she would end up. When I pressed her for details, she pulled back, noting that only if I was committed to action could she introduce me to her friend who might share her plan. It was an intriguing idea, and I filed it away for future reference."

"OK, I have to ask," Penny interrupted. "Do we call you Jai or George, Kay or Karma?"

"More on that directly. At this point in our romance we were still carrying birth names. When George rejected the $500,000 and learned from his secretary that the Chinese agent was extremely agitated and, in fact, threatened violence, we expedited our planned exit. I went straight to my friend, explained our general dilemma and the threats, and begged her for the contact information of her close friend. She asked me to leave the room and I assumed called her. When I was invited back in, my friend motioned for me to sit and advised me that she was in fact the actual contact, and if I was serious about needing to escape a dangerous situation, she could deliver me to a hideaway as early as the next morning. I said I was. She advised me to go

home and pack suitcases full of clothing to satisfy basic needs and be back by 6 a.m. I did, and we were."

"So, let me get this straight. You committed on the spot to run away to points unknown on the recommendation of a friend who hadn't been straight with you to give up everything you owned, including George's successful business and, of course, the half-million dollars, and turn it around in a matter of hours?" asked Penny in disbelief. "And you and George weren't even married?"

"Isn't that in essence what you and Sammy have done, Penny?" responded Kay.

Penny thought before responding. "I guess so."

"Things are just things. It was not hard to leave them behind. George knew that he could rebuild his business if he had to in Spring Town or somewhere else. What we knew we couldn't risk was losing each other."

"We can relate," noted Sammy.

"Well, we showed up at 6 a.m. as instructed, threw our bags in the trunk of my friend's car, and bid our old lives goodbye. As we pulled out, my friend asked again if we were sure we wanted to do this. When I nodded yes, she leaked a tear and indicated that she was envious."

"My friend explained that she was taking us deep into the Mark Twain National Forest to live with a family affiliated with the Free People, a group of conscientious, self-sufficient, dropout objectors scattered about as family or friend units, and living off the land. She added that the upper reaches of Goose Creek had been sheltered from degradation by the large national forest acreage, which itself was protected from any form of industrial or agricultural development. It was much of what little remained of the old Ozarks. Firewood provided heat, springs and shallow wells could be filtered to potable, and river baths assured personal hygiene. Wild game and vegetable gardens, supplemented by periodic trips to random grocery stores for canned goods and medical supplies, all under the disguise of normalcy, kept bellies full and bodies healthy. She called it an 'idyllic existence.' And it is."

"Is anyone unhappy here?" Sammy asked hesitantly.

"No one that I am aware of, and if they become so, they can simply drop back into the degraded society they left behind."

"What if they blow your cover?"

"What's to cover? We don't hurt anyone. Why would someone want to harm us?"

"Good point. Please continue," urged Penny.

"The family my friend initially settled us with were young, with two toddlers in tow. They lived in a relatively large—compared to this—self-constructed log cabin. They welcomed us with open arms, though it was clear that we would need to build our own place to have any privacy. Which we did, as you can see. They went by Panther and Slick and had given their children seasonal names, Winter and Summer."

"Is this when you decided to adopt your new names?"

"Yep, they were the only vestiges of the past we left behind. I chose Karma because it denotes peace and goodwill to me. Jai just liked the sound of his. Rhymed with 'guy' or something like that."

They all laughed at that.

"When are you due, Karma? Who will help you with delivery?"

"There is a male nurse who lives about a mile upstream from us, also along the creek. Buck knows that my water will be breaking soon and has promised to be on call the moment contractions begin."

"Is this your first birth, Karma? Are you scared?"

"Yes ...and no. I have talked to others Buck has worked with, and apart from normal delivery discomfort, there have been no problems. Buck assures me that my age won't be a major factor. Enough about us. We've carried on for far too long. Tell us your story, Penny and Sammy."

Two hours later all were intimately acquainted, though Penny and Sammy excluded details of their unusual circumstance and exit.

Chapter Twenty-Seven

NAMES

"**D**o you know the name of the lady lawyer who hustled us out of harm's way, Karma?" Penny asked as they were sipping coffee around the big fireplace one chilly morning. Several days had passed since Penny and Sammy had arrived, and they were settling into a reasonably comfortable, if crowded, pattern of daily living.

"Yes, I do, Penny, but I am not at liberty to share with you. Nothing personal, but them's the rules."

"Why am I not surprised?" Penny responded with a laugh. "No one knows anything about names, do they? It dawned on me that I haven't even said 'thank you' to her for saving our lives."

"She knows, dear Penny, she knows. She is the same one who saved ours and the only other time I have spoken to her since that early morning when she drove us to Panther and Slick's humble abode was when she called to ask if she could deliver you to us. The reason I know her name is that she was that prior friend who shed her anonymity to help us escape, and I am sworn to secrecy. It is not so much our fear of what harm some might bring out here because of our novel lifestyle, but what those in power could do to her if they found that she was an operative for the resistance on the ground."

"What do you mean, Karma? Operative? Resistance?"

"I don't fully know. Only that she is imbedded in something that runs much deeper and more profound than we are. At least that is what Jai and I intuit. The words are of my own choosing. You will get the sense when spring comes and we gather as a Free People with our unelected but unquestioned leader Maya that there is more going on than meets the eye."

"I know enough about the other side of the equation, those in power as you call them, to hope that there is a genuine resistance movement in play. Do you know anything about the Posse as they refer to themselves, Karma?"

"No. Never heard of it."

"Well, Sammy is, or was, a member of a clandestine group of activists who would sneak around select hog CAFOs in the middle of the night on text message orders from an unknown source and shoot an even dozen of the poor imprisoned beasts dead. Sammy called it 'messaging the man' that his desecration of our waters, air, land, and lifestyle was not going unnoticed. It was one of these Posse raids that got Sammy and me in such trouble. I don't know if I should be telling you this with all the secrets that are being kept on both sides of the aisle. Can I trust you, Karma?"

"Yes, Penny. You can trust Jai and me with anything, including your lives."

"I know, I know. You are saving our lives by hiding us out and sharing your lives with us. I'm sorry, Karma. I should never have asked you such a stupid question. Should I wait until Jai and Sammy get back from their hunt to tell all?

"Yes, please bring us into your world together."

"OK, but I do know this with all certainty, Karma. If there is a formal resistance movement, Sammy and I want to be part of it."

"So, Agent Smiley, that is where we are in the murder investigation. We believe we know who did it and suspect they may have committed another in conjunction with the theft of top secret government documents."

"What are their names, Sheriff Silas?"

"Ms. Penny Plumb—"

"Remember she spells her last name without a 'b,' Sheriff. P-l-u-m."

"Thanks, Deak, I always have trouble with that, but I enjoyed how it pissed her off when I mispronounced it. She even threatened to spit in my face that last time I did it. Anyway, Ms. Plum is a recent transplant from back East according to her employment file, though she claims deep Ozarks roots. Her boyfriend, Sammy Spode, is a local, born and bred of hillbilly half-breeds, whose claim to fame is as a fixer-upper. Makes, or made, his living that way. Our theory is that these two renegades killed a couple of CAFO owner Jimmy Johnson's pigs for no reason at all. He caught them in the act and shot the girl before one of them shot him dead. The other possible murder involves the local newspaper editor as the victim, and Plum and Spode as suspects in the theft of top secret documents. We have no idea what their motive was in any of this."

"Tell me about the secret documents, Sheriff."

"He can't, Agent Smiley," responded Archibald, "under the authority of one ranking higher than you or me. Must be some pretty powerful secret stuff, but our job is just to find the stash and return in to its rightful agent."

"Which agency might that be, Av?"

"I can't say, Agent Smiley. We need your help in tracking down Plum and Spode, which is the extent of our charge. You are reputed to have an excellent record in finding suspects who have fled justice, and that is what we need from you today. Any ideas on where we should turn next?"

"Actually, I do, Av. You say a key piece of evidence in your suppositions is the wound you believe Ms. Plum received the night of the first murder. You also state that you have checked with every hospital emergency room and every doctor in the region to try and determine who might have treated a serious gunshot wound that evening and have found nothing.'

"Correct, Agent Smiley, correct."

"Have you thought about extending your search to dentists, even veterinarians, in the likelihood that there might be a friendship between one of the suspects and a medical professional of sorts who might have provided emergency treatment?"

"No, but that's a wonderful idea," chimed in Av. "This is why we wanted your input. Brilliant, don't you think, Sheriff?"

Sheriff Silas shrugged in weak concurrence. This was not the way he thought or reasoned. "Thanks for the idea, Agent Smiley. I will put together a list of dentists and vets in the community and cross-check them with the suspects for age, shared interests, or acquaintances and any kind of common bond. Shouldn't be that difficult. And if we do stumble onto any kind of a match, my deputies and I will follow up with personal interrogation."

"Thanks to you and the FBI, Agent Smiley, for your assistance," added Av. "We will keep you posted on any progress and check back periodically. Goodbye."

Av looked at Sheriff Silas and smiled. "You do the ground-work, Sheriff, but if you find someone who might fit the image of an accomplice, you will turn the information over to me. I have access to professionals who are trained in extracting information from even the most reluctant witnesses. They will conduct the follow-up interviews. Let me know if you come up with any potential matches sheriff as soon as possible."

Penny and Sammy shared the rest of their story with Jai and Karma around the warm fireplace with hot coffee and total frankness. And in promised confidence. They began with the exchange of gunfire at the Johnson pig CAFO, the shooting of the owner in self-defense after he had wounded Penny, the trip to a dear veterinarian friend to treat her bullet wounds, and the subsequent suspicion it aroused with Penny's boss. They followed with the editor's death and Penny's discovery of a treasure trove of classified documents in his office near his dead body. They shared a summary view of A Coalition for Prosperity's vast international conspiracy to control meat production around the world at the expense of family farmers and natural resources subjected to corporate industrial farming. They closed with how close they came to being detained as prime suspects in a murder and secret document theft before being rescued by Karma's friend.

Jai and Karma sat spellbound through the whole narrative, unable to totally grasp the enormity of it all, yet starting to sense links to what was happening in their new brave world. They reiterated their pledge of confidentiality.

"We also need to share with you some critical connecting information if you are willing. Having such knowledge could carry great risk," Penny added.

Both nodded their concurrence.

Penny reached under her heavy wool sweater and pulled out the keys attached to her gold necklace. "We have stored all of the top secret information in two safe deposit boxes at the Spring Town Community Bank. This is one of two sets of keys to access. Our friend Richard, the Posse member veterinarian who treated my wound, has the other set until your friend, the still unnamed one who helped us escape, can find someone trustworthy to review, validate, and figure out how best to use the documentation to stop this madness. It is our belief, though not yet confirmed, that bank president Jarrod Combs is also a Posse member. If anything happens to us, dead or alive, you need to secure these keys for your friend."

Both Jai and Karma nodded warily. "How long do you think it will take for all of this to play out, Penny, for the documents to go public, for the conspiracy to be confronted and eliminated, for order to return to the Ozarks?"

"No idea, Jai. No earthly idea. Maybe never, who knows? I would hope that Karma's friend will have gotten the safe deposit box keys from Richard, but I can't even be certain about that. She promised not to make a move on the contents until she had the people and processes in place to handle efficiently and thoroughly. I just know that we cannot lose control of those documents, or Sammy and I will have no last line of defense personally, and this travesty can go on forever."

—⚇—

"So, Penny, are you and Sammy going to lose your God-given names in favor of ones more suited to your new lifestyle?" Karma asked with a smile the next morning.

"Names, names, names," mumbled Penny. "Some won't share them, some change them, some hide behind them. It's a strange time to have a name." She looked at Sammy as if perplexed.

Sammy spoke up immediately. "The only name I want to change is Penny's last one."

Penny smiled back at Sammy. "Well that can be done. And we may need another Sammy," she said, patting her belly. "I'm two months past my last period and am feeling stuffed."

Chapter Twenty-Eight

MISSING LINKS

"**K**arma, I need to talk to Penny immediately."

Karma handed the phone to Penny with a concerned look on her face.

It was Karma's friend who had rescued Penny and Sammy. "Richard is missing, Penny. His wife says that he has simply disappeared. She evidently got my number from his cell phone contact list under 'Posse.' Have you heard anything from him since your escape?"

"No. Oh no. No one knows where he is? Have you gotten the keys from him yet?"

"No. I have been having trouble assembling the team I need to process the contents of the boxes, and my superiors are leery of releasing the documents from your protective custody until I do. That is a whole another story, but for now, everything should be as you left it."

"Your superiors? What does that mean? Does anyone know where Richard's keys are?"

"No."

—m—

"I think we've got a link, Av." It was Sheriff Silas on the line with Avarice Archibald, confirming that he had a legitimate suspect for whom had treated Penny Plum's wound. "In running through our community list of veterinarians, I have discovered one Dr. Richard Bloom. He is roughly the age of murder suspect Sammy Spode and is known to have hung out with him per several of their mutual friends. He is also actively involved in several local environmental groups."

"Sounds like our man, Sheriff. Good work. I will have my folks pay the good doctor a visit tomorrow and see if he is willing to cooperate."

As Doctor Richard sat in his office, which was situated next to his residence, reviewing the file of an elderly German Shepherd whose owners were reticent to put him down, the doorbell rang.

"Lucy?" he asked before remembering that she had gone into town to shop. He rose and unlocked the door, opening it for an elderly couple who carried a small poodle and inviting them in.

"Are you Dr. Bloom?" the old man asked in a soft voice.

"Yes, Dr. Richard Bloom. How can I help you?"

The old lady handed the poodle to Richard, who turned and carried it into the exam room, paying no attention to the two owners who were throwing clothes, wigs, and disguises into a pile before following him in.

"What seems to be the problem with your lovable dog?"

"The only problems we are aware of are those that will befall you if you do not cooperate with our investigation into the murder of Jimmy Johnson," answered a gruff voice.

Richard turned amidst the alarm bells going off in his brain to face two withering stares from unforgiving eyes, two weapons pointed at his chest, and one order to sit down. One of the young thugs locked the door behind them while the other pulled up a chair and sat directly in front of Richard, just inches from his face.

"OK, I'm going to say this once and once only. I intend to kill you slowly and painfully if you do not answer my questions fully and honestly."

—⟶⟵—

"Your friend Richard is dead, Penny. Authorities found him early this morning with his neck wrapped in a barbed wire fence in a field outside his office."

Penny shrieked and ran to get Sammy, carrying the phone. Sammy was nowhere to be found, out hunting again. The call from Karma's friend, the one who had rescued Penny and Sammy and still would not share her name, sent Penny into overload. She screamed into the phone, "Goddamnit, what is your name, and what is going on? Richard is dead? What about Lucy? What about the keys? What about our papers? What about Sammy and me? What about—what's next?"

—⚏—

"So how do I cover this up, Av? No bad news, right? What could be worse than a locally respected veterinarian found strangled in barbed wire in his own back forty? How is that going to help business?"

"I know, Sheriff, I know. My boys evidently got a little carried away when the vet wouldn't even acknowledge their questions and, according to them, spat in their faces at some point. He evidently passed out while they had him in a choke hold, and they couldn't revive him. Since he had marks around his neck, they needed to cover those up and tried to make it look like an accident."

"Av, forgive me, but what kind of idiots would think that someone could accidentally strangle themselves on a barbed wire fence in their own backyard? And this after the idiots evidently carted him around for a couple of days trying to figure out how to cover their tracks. All they accomplished was adding undo confusion to a missing-person-found-murdered case. What in the hell were they thinking, Av?"

"I know, I know."

"And it didn't help that the body was found by a neighbor and close friend. He and his wife are scared to death and demanding a full and timely investigation. They want to know if they are under imminent threat."

"Well, make something up, Sheriff. Come up with a credible explanation. And tell your friend Deak not to cover the story in his newspaper. Got it?"

"Yes, sir."

"And we need to get somebody in the vet's office and house to go through it for any clues as to how to track down Plumb and her running mate. They must be close if he chose to die rather than provide information."

"It doesn't sound like he had much choice about anything with your goons, Av."

"Point taken. Anyway, can you manage to have some of your folks search the office and house without arousing too much suspicion? Maybe just tell his wife you need to do so to certify it was an accidental death and not a murder or a suicide?"

"Suicide by strangling oneself with barbed wire? Come on, Av. Maybe looking for clues that he was killed but no more."

"Whatever you can come up with, Sheriff. I don't even know what we are looking for, but we've got to go through this part, Sheriff, in case we can find something to link or lead us to the real suspects."

—∿—

"Settle, Penny, settle. We need to think clearly and quickly. I am truly sorry about your friend Richard. We are dealing with powerful forces, and he fell victim to them for helping you. We don't know whether they got the keys to the safe deposit boxes, but we can't assume that they didn't. Which means we need to transfer the contents to another safe harbor now, today. And, my name is Lynda, Penny. Lynda Leopold. You deserve to know after all you have been through. I'm on your side, along with the organization I represent. I will share more when we have time, but right now you need to move those documents to another safe haven. The man who delivered you to Jai and Karma will be by to get you in an hour. I will meet you at the bank, and we will pretend not to know one another, though I will inform President Combs about what we are up to. You will transfer all documents to your backpack and leave it in the ladies' room. I will follow you in and take it with me to a safe I have access to in my superior's office. I will leave it there until I get the processing team assembled. Come alone, Penny. You will be returned to Sammy directly from the bank."

"I don't like this, Lynda. I will be giving up total control over the only thing that can potentially protect Sammy and me in the event we are ever caught. Those papers provide the only context that can put in perspective our unfortunate encounter with violence and the scar on my arm. Richard fired back in self-defense after I had been wounded. It was not murder unless butchering pigs is, and these conspiratorial maniacs are doing that by the thousands each day and getting rich from it. They are also murdering our water, our air—"

"Slow down, Penny. Deep breath. Think through this. You trusted me, a total stranger, to hustle you and Richard off to a strange place deep in the Ozark wilderness. You trusted me to share possession of the explosive documents that we are at risk of losing control over now. You must trust me again. What is the alternative?"

Several days later the sheriff was on the phone with Av again. "She let us go through things in the hope of finding something that leads to his attacker. She is convinced it was murder, likely to get some of the doc's narcotics. I tried to get Bloom's cell phone, but she claimed that it was lost along the way. Never did find it. I promised to share anything we found that could support her theory. She is obviously very distraught and in no mood to write this off as an accident. Similar to the mood of her neighbors. All are very frightened. Point being I did find something of interest. In the office desk drawer were two safe deposit box keys, with consecutive numbers on them. They would have to belong to the Spring Town Community Bank, wouldn't you think?"

"Definitely. I believe you and I should inspect these boxes personally, Sheriff. Together. When can we meet there? "

"Two hours?"

"See you then, Sheriff."

There was no headline in the *Spring Town Gazette*. There was no story. Only an obituary announcing that young Spring Town veterinarian Richard Bloom had lost his life in a tragic accident just outside his home. Nor was there any mention of the nature of the accident, the time he was missing, or the possibility of foul play.

Lucy Bloom was beside herself but feeling powerless against a corrupt law enforcement establishment and lying local press. She would have to take her case elsewhere and would lean on Richard's Posse contact to help her.

"It's empty, Av. This damn box is flat-out empty."

"Try the other one, Sheriff."

"Same, Av. Nothing in it."

"So, we have two oversized safe deposit boxes, which obviously cost a fair amount, sitting empty, with no indication of usage. We've got to see who the boxes are registered to and what kind of recent activity there has been. My guess is that they belong to our prime suspects, who were storing our secret documents for someone or some group to go through and expose A Coalition of Prosperity. That Plum and Spode somehow got wind that we had a key and moved quickly to relocate. That must mean they are somewhere close by and have been in touch with Bloom's wife. We need to intensify our local search effort for both them and the documents. Do you know the president of this bank, Sheriff?"

"Yes. Jarrod Combs. Kind of an odd duck. We—Deak and me—could never get him to play along with us. We really didn't need him because of the Coalition's sophisticated international funds management system, but I always thought he was aware of more than he shared."

"Sheriff, you need to talk to him as soon as possible about the renter of these boxes and obtain a record of activity. There may even be an address or contact information attached."

"Well, how about right now? He's rarely busy. Meet you back at your office."

Sheriff headed to the corner office in the bank, where he found President Combs hunched over some paperwork at his desk. He bypassed the secretary and went straight to the open door.

"Morning, Jarrod. Do you have a minute to visit? I've got some important questions to ask and need your assistance."

"Sure, Sheriff Silas, come right in and have a seat."

"I need information about the two large safe deposit boxes these keys access," the sheriff said handing the keys to Combs. "Things like who they are registered to, a log of recent activity, contact information for the renters, and anything related. This is part of a murder investigation, Jarrod."

Combs looked over the keys, examined the numbers, and asked Sheriff Slack where he had obtained them.

"Can't really say, Jarrod, confidential information."

"Well, Sheriff, not sure where these keys came from, but those two boxes, which are our largest, haven't been rented for months. Too expensive for most locals."

Chapter Twenty-Nine

BORED

Danny Dufford was bored, really bored. From his early days with a large independent Midwestern newspaper, he had tackled every day, every assignment, every story with an energy, a curiosity, a reckless abandon, and an intensity befitting the high-end journalism degree he had earned. He had found no problem gaining a good job upon graduation and performing at a high level when given the opportunity. And that was the problem—when given an opportunity.

After five years and countless personal awards, his paper had been acquired by a media conglomerate, operations and editorial opinion centralized, and staff laid off or bought out.

No longer allowed to create and pursue his own writing agenda, he was now told what to cover and how to report it by some idiot whom he had never met halfway across the country.

Another problem was the fact that general consolidation of media outlets and independent publishers was accelerating in the face of digital competition and declining subscribers. His generation simply didn't want to take the time to sit down and read a thorough, well-written, controversial full-page story when they could pick up the daily headlines on their smartphone. So, when Danny tried to take his passion and skill set elsewhere, the story was generally the same. "We tell you what to cover, how to do it, and what to write. If that is acceptable, you have a position at a salary less than what you started at straight out of J-school."

At the depth of his disillusionment, he got a strange call from a total stranger straight out of the blue. She claimed to have read a piece he had written several years back about climate change that had been intelligent, insightful, and passionate, and she was impressed. She had followed his career and the many awards he had garnered and wondered if that left any time in his busy career to take on special projects. She couldn't pay much but thought he might find the subject matter intriguing, perhaps even award-deserving.

He could barely disguise his enthusiasm as they talked in generalities, and she suggested she drive to meet him at his earliest convenience.

"What's your name, ma'am?"

"I'd rather tell you in person, Mr. Dufford."

—m—

"He's lying to you, Sheriff. They don't allow spare keys that work on a box to be floating around for months. He is in cahoots with them and perhaps something much bigger than just them."

"I agree with you, Av. But promise me that you won't send your handpicked goons to find out. I've covered up so much shit from their last expedition that I may never stand on solid ground again."

"Maybe it's time to bring in Agent Smiley again? He had a damn good idea last time around, not one I would have thought of. Maybe he can jump-start us again."

—m—

"Hi, Mr. Dufford, I'm Lynda, Lynda Leopold."

"Nice to meet you, Ms. Leopold. Is it Ms. or Mrs.? And how did you know it was me?"

"You are the only young handsome dude in this bar, as far as I can see. And it is Ms., but please call me Lynda."

"Only if you reciprocate with Danny."

"Let's grab a table and a drink. I think you are going to want one after you hear my proposal."

"Let me help you with your backpack, Lynda."

"Not just yet, Danny. We need to talk before you touch that!"

—⟁—

Penny and Sammy and Jai and Karma sat around Lucy, embracing her when she occasionally burst in tears. Lucy had found them through Richard's Posse contact after she had called for help.

Lynda, who did not reveal her name to Lucy, advised that she would be sending someone to pick her up to connect with them. Lucy needed to trust her on this. Lynda was going to be out of town for a few days and would try to come join them when she returned. She hoped to have very important news to share at that time.

They listened in stunned silence as Lucy tried to get her story out. About Richard disappearing for a couple of days, about the neighbors eventually finding him strangled to death on a barbed wire fence on the property behind their house and office, about Sheriff Slack refusing to call it anything more than an accident— despite the time Richard was missing and without conducting a full investigation, about the *Spring Town Gazette's* refusal to publish anything more than a carefully worded obituary, about—

"There is clearly another cover-up going on here," burst out Penny. "Lucy, we are so sorry to have dragged you and Richard into this tragic situation. We have learned more about a sinister international conspiracy than you will ever want to know in your time of loss. Just know that this is bigger than us and that your loss can be avenged if we play our hand carefully. I have to ask, did Richard ever tell you about two safe deposit boxes, the keys that went with them, or the contents thereof?"

"No." Lucy sobbed again.

"So, you don't have any idea where the keys might be or if the sheriff and his lackeys might have found them?"

"No, but he did search Richard's office and our house, purportedly looking for evidence that Richard had been murdered. He promised to keep me informed of any finding but claimed to have none when he left. What a liar."

"You don't know the half of it, Lucy."

—⟁—

Two hours and six beers between them later, Lynda let Danny touch the backpack. She had begun their conversation with the admonition that under no circumstances was Danny to pass along any of the information she was about to share with him. She didn't know him well enough to fully trust him, but all she had read or heard pointed to a brilliant journalist and stand-up guy.

Two separate contacts in the newspaper business to whom she had been referred by her national environmental organization had confirmed such a profile. She had needed to meet him in person and trust her instincts if she felt that to be true. She warned him that she had copies of all the key documents she would pass along to him, which was a lie. But Lynda was at a desperate stage in this drama and needed to hold on to a trump card or two in case she had mis-judged the man.

Lynda explained to Danny that she had reams of legitimate documentation of a sinister international conspiracy that was wreaking havoc on the world order and the global environment. She was a member of an opposition resistance that could be wiped out if their identity was compromised, which is why securing Danny's pledge of confidentially was vital to sharing more. His hand was shaking slightly when he extended it, grasped hers. He nodded.

Lynda explained that time was of the essence, as one innocent party to their efforts had already been brutally murdered, and others were in hiding. She had originally hoped to organize a team of resistance insiders to methodically sift through the contents of her backpack but had not really found the experience or the talent to review, absorb, organize, and strategize on going public.

"These are the very things that I have done all my life, Lynda."

"That is why I am here, Danny. My supervisor finally signed off on this huge gamble on you as the enemy creeps ever closer to tracking us down."

"Who is your supervisor?"

"I can't tell you, Danny."

"How did you get all this, Lynda?"

"Two brave souls stole it and ultimately entrusted it to me—and now to you. All of our lives are at risk."

"Where are you spending the night, Lynda?"

"I was planning on driving back tonight, but given the beers, I think I'll just grab a cheap motel room on the way out of town and head back tomorrow."

"You will do nothing of the kind, Lynda. I want you to follow me to my apartment, get some sleep, and wake up early to join me in attacking this treasure trove. I promise I will not accost you, even though you are a very beautiful woman, and will give you the fullest privacy a two-bedroom apartment can afford. Let's go so we can get rested then started."

"OK, Danny. Thank you, and thanks for the compliment," Lynda added with a wink.

Chapter Thirty

A MARATHON

When Lynda crawled out of her bed, it was still dark outside, but there was a light showing through under the door she had kept locked all night. She cracked it and saw Danny hunched over his kitchen table, sorting papers and files left and right.

"Mornin," she squeaked.

"Mornin, beautiful."

"Even though I did spend the night with you, Mr. Dufford, you don't know me well enough to address me as such."

"Whoops. I'm sorry, but can we not go back to the Ms. and Mr. stage?"

Lynda smiled and nodded.

"How do you know all of this is real, Lynda? That it comes from trustworthy sources? I've barely scratched the surface, but this reads like a cheap paperback novel, too random and bizarre to even dream up. Help yourself to coffee," he added, pointing to a Keurig on the sideboard.

After a cup and a half in total silence, as Danny kept shuffling and stacking, Lynda announced that she had better be headed home.

"No," Danny almost pleaded. "I need you here with me, Lynda. This is simply too much for a single soul to take in alone."

"I've got others that need me, Danny. The widow of our slain colleague is hiding out with the ones who provided these source documents. She doesn't know what to do about a corrupt sheriff who refuses to investigate her husband's death as a homicide or a fake news gazette that reports nothing but pap to the local population. I have one who I rescued due to deliver her first baby any day now, and two others who will need to find alternative housing when the baby arrives. And I have a supervisor who is anxiously awaiting my report on meeting with you."

"I need you more, Lynda, and if you insist on leaving, I will tell your damn super that you shacked up with me the first night we met, which can't be good for your credibility. Please stay, Lynda," Danny continued to insist.

Three nights later, a little after midnight, Lynda and Danny finally rolled into bed. Together. Both could feel it coming as they did little but read, talk, eat, and sleep.

Lynda had watched with deepening admiration as Danny organized and digested page after page of documents, file after file of records and cash trails, photograph after photograph of compromised officials, filling a whole legal pad with notes and connecting lines. He was tireless and indistractable.

She had called in to explain her extended absence and assure her people that the project was on track and moving forward. She even validated it with a name, "Posse Tracks." She spoke briefly with Karma to reassure that she would be around to help when the baby arrived.

When Lynda and Danny had finally taken a night off to just talk and enjoy Lynda's cooking, one bottle of wine had turned into two and two bodies connected as one.

As they lay together next morning, Danny asked where the "Posse Tracks" moniker had come from. Lynda thought the "Tracks" part was pretty evident, and Danny nodded in agreement. Her attempt to explain "Posse" sent Danny into howls of laughter.

"You mean, you have organized this group of men, young and old, who sally forth in the middle of the night at the ping of a text from you to shoot and kill a dozen confined pigs each for purposes of sending a message to the man?"

"There are a few women too."

—⟋⟍—

"We've been summoned to the assistant secretary's office, gentlemen," announced Av grimly. "He has apparently gotten wind of what has been going on down here in little old Spring Town and is not happy. Multiple murders. Missing top secret documents. Disappearing suspects. Lying bank presidents. It has become more than a hiccup I fear. We are to fly to Washington tomorrow for an unknown length of stay."

"Do you think we should go, Av? I mean they're not going to hurt us or kill us are they? Most of this has been out of our control, don't you think? Do we have to go?" whined Deacon Duncan.

"Maybe there will be one of those pig bureau seminars with the pretty ladies to cheer us up?" added Sheriff Silas hopefully.

"I think my water just broke, Jai. And it's starting to feel uncomfortable."

Chapter Thirty-One

TIGHTENING....

"**P**ush, Karma, push" urged Buck, whom Sammy had fetched while Jai, Lynda, and Penny tended to Karma. Warmed towels and steaming water lay spread across the kitchen table in some semblance of order. Penny held one of Karma's hands, Lynda the other. Sammy looked on in the horror of knowing he would soon be in the middle of something like this.

Mom moaned, baby emerged in silence and then issued a high-pitched cry signaling life.

"You have a handsome baby boy, Karma. He looks healthy in every respect."

"I'm so happy," she sighed, as Jai beamed.

"Let me cut the cord and clean him just a bit, and he will be yours to hold."

—⟶⟵—

Danny Dufford wasn't about to let Lynda leave without him. They had grown close in a very short period of time and were both honed in on "Posse Tracks." Lynda didn't want to leave Danny either but had to get home to cover all the other needs awaiting.

Perhaps Danny could finish his screening of the materials under the cover of Lynda's apartment in Spring Town. Both knew that it was risky even being near a local power structure that was intent on finding and terminating them and their work. And this was even before the stakes were being raised dramatically in Washington, unknown to them.

Lynda considered requesting permission for Danny's placement with the Free People but decided that she had dumped more than enough risk on them the past month with Penny and Sammy. No, their lifestyle and secrets must be protected at all cost. She would see to that.

Plus, she enjoyed his company. She had survived serious relationships in the past and wasn't sure she wanted another just now, but a little fun and pleasure never hurt anyone. And she was intrigued with his work ethic and organizational competence. If anyone could pull this multitentacled plot together for public consumption, she had the feeling it could be Danny. And, big picture-wise, nothing she was involved with was more critical to the future of the Ozarks.

Maybe it was time to bring in Maya to bless the choices she was making.

"Gentlemen, the assistant secretary will see you now."

Avarice Archibald, Deacon Duncan, and Sheriff Silas Slack were led down a long poorly lit corridor to an isolated conference room that obviously had several entry points. A short, fat, balding man whose real name was Sonny entered the room opposite from the Spring Town delegation. He greeted Av warmly and simply shook hands with the other two.

"Av, you have always been one of my most trusted lieutenants. How have you gotten us into such a mess? Is it these guys' fault? You gentlemen know that you have put our whole international movement at risk. Av has informed me that you know all of the inner workings and pressure points and have lost documentation which could destroy us all if it becomes public. And even more disturbing, a couple of young redneck refugees have simply disappeared from sight along with this top secret information. I called you here to find out what you intend to do about this dramatic breach in security."

Av spoke first. "We don't believe our documents have been compromised, Mr. Assistant Secretary. At least not yet. We know they have been moved about several times and continue to believe that ultimate knowledge and control reside with the two suspects in the murder of prominent Spring Town citizen and CAFO owner Jimmy Johnson. Our focus has and will continue to be on finding Penny Plum and Sammy Spode, reclaiming the docs from them, and eliminating them and any memory of them from existence."

"What about the other murder, Av? My intelligence tells me that it was the result of a botched interrogation gone haywire. That is was unnecessary and poorly conceived, executed, and covered up."

"I must take responsibility for that, Mr. Assistant Secretary. I employed a team of interrogators who came highly recommended by one of my peers in the network. They panicked when they lost control and never fully recovered their senses. Sheriff Slack did the best he could with what he had to work with."

"Let's put aside blame for the moment and talk about solutions," interrupted the assistant secretary. "And consequences."

"So, Sheriff Slack, what is your plan if we allow you to return to Spring Town and attempt to bring closure to this case?"

"Allow, Mr. Assistant Secretary?"

"Yes, allow, Sheriff Slack. You might consider yourself a prisoner seeking parole at the moment."

Sheriff looked at Deak and then Av in confusion before responding. "Well, it is our intention to consult with FBI Agent Smiley and seek his advice in tracking down the suspects. He was very helpful with the last consultation, recommending that we expand our medical provider pool to include veterinarians and finding one who even had a direct connection with the suspects."

"You mean the one you had murdered?"

There was only silence in the tense room.

"Stay away from Smiley. Does everyone understand that? He knows too much already, and I don't trust him not to leak it to his colleagues. You can do better than that, Slack. My intelligence tells me that Plum and Spode are more than rogue operators in a dangerous game, gentlemen. Tell me about the precisely planned assassination of CAFO livestock. Who is organizing and executing that? Is there a clandestine vigilante group at work here? Have you thought about broadening your net before it's too late?"

"Great idea, Mr. Assistant Secretary. May we have access to your intelligence to help guide our efforts?"

"Yes, of course, Av. What else are you going to do?"

"I guess we need to gather information on every environmental group on the ground, whether national-, state-, or local-based. And investigate every member, every activist, every relation thereto. We'll build a 'hit list' to aggressively research and question personally when appropriate.

"Now you're thinking, Av. Thinking strategically, like the Av I know and trust. The problem, gentlemen, is that you don't really have much time to execute your plans. Thirty days to be precise to get those documents back under our control."

The three Spring Towners looked at each other in confusion. "Or what?" mumbled Av.

"Well, Sheriff Slack here could become the new sheriff of a Uyghur Muslim reeducation camp in the Xinjiang region of Northwest China, and Deacon Duncan could launch another paper, the *Yining County Gazette*, to provide coverage of China's efforts to bring poor Muslims into the modern economy. And incidentally, both of you would need to attend said reeducation camp to learn proper Mandarin Chinese before assuming your new leadership roles. At least they wouldn't be alone halfway around the world. We Coalition for Prosperity partners cooperate in many ways."

The sheriff outwardly cringed, Deak stared bleakly at the ceiling.

"And you, Av, reckon we would bring you back to DC for internal retraining. You know too much to let out of our sights. Of course, this is all just hypothetical, if you can just get those top secret documents back where they belong in thirty days."

Chapter Thirty-Two

MAYA

Maya lived in a modest cabin, deeper in the forest than the others.

Maya's background was shrouded in mystery. No one knew when she came to the forest. Or the Ozarks. Nor did they know her age, her lineage, her roots. They understood only her charisma, her passion, and her compassion. And that drew them to her, kept them attached, and inspired them to think on a higher plane.

Some thought of Maya in mystical, even mythological, terms. Was she of this world or another, one asked. Was she put here for us or us for her or we for each, wondered another. Did she have lovers or friends, confidants or cohabiters? No one knew because she was always alone when leading. And frankly no one cared because she seemed to care for all equally.

Those who knew her best did her bidding without asking. They knew that deep inside her burned a fierce desire to reclaim the beauty and health of the Ozarks for the natural heirs, by any means or methods required.

Maya's network consisted of her People, her activists on the ground, and a small layer of trusted field operatives between. Simple, lean, loyal. Maya had become the face of the resistance. Others planned. Others executed. But when Maya appeared, when Maya beamed outward, when Maya spoke, the Free People listened.

—◊◊◊—

"Maya, meet Danny, meet Penny and Sammy," said Lynda softly. "They are the latest recruits in the struggle to reclaim the Ozarks."

Chapter Thirty-Three

DRAGNET

"**W**elcome, friends," Maya greeted each with a sustained and warm hug.

"I have been briefed on what you have done to aide our cause, and I am truly grateful, as are Free People everywhere. You have taken risks, faced dangers, and stood up to the man and his plan to plunder the Ozarks and its peoples. Thank you. The question becomes what can we do next? Penny and Sammy, the information you have provided would seem to substantiate our deepest fears. A plot, a conspiracy, a worldwide web of deceit and deception driven and sustained by greed and money, an insatiable thirst for power, and the basest self-serving instincts. A Coalition for Prosperity might sound noble on the surface, but at its rotten core is no more than a bloated sense of self, a pus-filled, oozing wound when barely scratched on the surface."

All leaned closer as Maya's fury burst forth in a torrent of words and emotions. None had ever sensed such anger, such indignation, such repulsion, such passion, such resolve. It was catching.

Sheriff Silas, Deak Duncan, and Avarice Archibald sat hunched in despair around the editor's desk at the *Spring Town Gazette*.

"We've got to get our hands on those damn files, those secret papers, those photos and money laundering records. Forget about Plum and her squeeze. They will burn in hell for what they have done, for the murder of an innocent man, perhaps of even another. It's the papers that hold the key for us. No way I'm going to some far-out Chinese Muslim school to learn

Mandarin and start a newspaper," growled an indignant Deacon Duncan.

"I'm not going there either," added Sheriff Silas. "Maybe we ought to just disappear out in the woods, like that commune of hippies down along Goose Creek. I hear they wander around in the nude half the time and share their love freely. Might be as much fun as a pig bureau symposium, with all its fringes."

"Shut up, you idiots, both of you. I don't think you realize what serious trouble we are in. The assistant secretary and his entourage mean business and will do anything in the name of control. If you would rather die, I'm sure they can arrange that as well. You are correct, Deak. We have got to get our hands on those files within the next thirty—well, make that twenty-nine now—days. Sheriff, I suggest that you begin a wholesale roundup of any known environmental activists in Spring Town. Compile your list, bring them in for questioning one by one. I will personally handle the interrogations while you take notes, Deak, looking for any signs of entanglement in any kind of plot, from body language to excessive nervousness to defiance, and so on. Those who exhibit will be brought back in for another, shall we say, more intensive round of inquiry. We start today, gentlemen. Our futures, our lives are on the line. This is not a problem we can run from because they will find us. This is a problem we must solve ourselves.

"We need to get you in a different dwelling in the woods, Penny and Sammy," ordered Maya.

"Jai and Karma need some privacy with their new little one. Tonja and Tonio, have a pretty large cabin and lots of room, despite their two children. Would you mind moving there today, again temporarily, until we can set about building a permanent structure for you this spring? They have great access to water, a solid life routine, and live close to Jai and Karma. It's a relatively short walk, and he can show you the way. What do you think?"

"Sure, we will move our two suitcases as soon as we finish here."

"Lynda, your situation is more precarious. I don't think it is safe for you and Danny to even return to Spring Town with the papers. I am guessing the ones attempting to track you down at this point go far beyond the blubbering sheriff and his band of incompetents. What do you require in order to complete your work, Danny?" asked Maya.

"Well, to be honest, I need seclusion, except for Lynda here whom I depend on greatly for support and encouragement. I'm pretty close to pulling enough loose ends together to present a viable case. And that's the other thing I will soon need. Advice and counsel. In all of my analyzing and reporting of nefarious schemes and evil intentions, I have never encountered anything quite like this. Frankly, I'm not sure how to most effectively share it. Call a press conference? Go to a major metropolitan newspaper or TV channel for release? Write a lead story for the *New York Times* and see if they will run it? Go to the FBI or the CIA for cease and desist enforcement? Go to an independent nation not involved in the conspiracy and seek their intervention? Send a summary report to the assistant secretary of agriculture's office, with a threat to release if they don't disband and police themselves? I have always thought I am somewhat of an innovative media expert, but I'm not with something of this magnitude. I need help, Maya. I need help if we are to bring down this nefarious network without losing our lives or starting an international conflagration."

Maya set quietly for a while, obviously processing options in her head. No one moved.

"Okay, this is what I propose for you and Lynda, Danny. You will stay with me until our strategy is secure. I have a small extra bedroom attached the back of my cabin. Most don't even know it exists, let alone where to find me. Only my most trusted operatives, like Lynda, have direct access to me. No one must know you are here with me. I have never offered this before, but I simply can't think of a better short-term solution. Lynda, I sure some of my clothes will fit you, and I will arrange to pick up some rudimentary menswear, Danny, as soon as I can dream up a plausible excuse. I hope you both will find me a comfortable hostess as well as a creative source of ideas for proceeding further. That said, we must make this work. There is so much riding on it."

Lynda and Danny nodded their wide-eyed concurrence simultaneously.

—∿—

"Nothing suspicious yet among the ones I've brought in?"

"No, not really. Just keep bringing 'em, Sheriff. Something is bound to show."

"There is one conspicuous absence from my list of interviewees, Av. I can't seem to locate her anywhere or find anyone who can acknowledge her whereabouts."

"Who is that, Sheriff?"

"One Lynda Leopold."

Chapter Thirty-Four

WHAT NEXT?

As Penny and Sammy and Lynda and Danny settled into their new temporary quarters, the noose was tightening in Spring Town. Lynda's fellow field operative Lydia Latvia reported daily to Maya, through a third party, on the increasingly frantic efforts of local authorities to locate Lynda. An all-points bulletin had been issued and a significant monetary award posted for information that could lead to her whereabouts. Lydia had been detained and questioned twice as one who was identified as being acquainted with Lynda. The second time around was rougher, with threats of lie detector tests and incarceration tossed about. Someone or something was clearly turning up the heat. Maya was glad that Lydia didn't know anything about Lynda's temporary relocation location or the reason for it.

Lydia also reported that the community was abuzz about the recent suicide of Spring Town Community Bank President Jarrod Combs. He was found hanging from a ceiling fan in his office by his assistant before the bank opened, with no note or explanation to be found. The *Spring Town Gazette* put forth a front-page story opining that Combs had been involved in a major bank fraud involving cash and safe deposit boxes, keys to which had been discovered in his desk drawer.

Maya knew better.

Av was proud of his work and that of his henchmen.

Sammy asked Penny to marry him. Again. This while they lay in the afterglow of a brief shared moment, albeit a short one, as Tonja and Tonio had taken their two boys out to play in the woods.

"After all we've been together for a while, gotten ourselves in a heap of trouble together, and made a baby together. I think it's time to formally get together."

"I agree, Sammy, but not until we have some permanence in our lives, either here with the Free People, in a new town or space under aliases, or in jail."

They reclothed quickly as their hosts piled in from the cold outside.

—m—

"I think I've got enough to write a comprehensive expose on A Coalition for Prosperity and back my accusations with documentation and proven facts, Maya. It will include the big vision, the partners (international, national, and corporate), the operational structure, and the clandestine funding network. It will name names from the top down, link accounts and backdoor agreements, and count currencies. It is a tell-all, in-depth look at a rogue coalition of powerful players set on controlling world agricultural production and markets in the sole interest of self-enrichment, and at the expense of traditional farmers, innocent consumers, and local environments. It is an insidious plot against most of humankind on a scale never before attempted. And sadly, it is entrenched and working effectively and efficiently. No one outside the inner circle could ever have imagined such a conspiracy, and we wouldn't know today unless Penny and Sammy stumbling into one of the Coalition's operational backrooms and had the courage to dig deeper."

"Well done, Danny. What next?" asked Maya, as Lynda sat clinging to Danny's hand, and Penny and Sammy leaned into one another in front of the roaring fire in Maya's cabin.

"That's the problem, Maya, I just don't know. I'm a newspaper guy at heart with an inclination to find some organization to run the whole thing, spread the word on cable, radio, and social media, and see if the rest of the world will step up and in to bust up A Coalition for Prosperity.

"The biggest problem is not knowing whom to trust. In a media world of interlocking corporate interests, the cloud of 'fake news' hanging over most attempts at honest journalism and the physical risks associated with revealing our faces and showing our hand, I don't know where to turn. This is where I need help, Maya. You are a wise and passionate human being, and I need your guidance before moving forward. I fear for all of our lives when, and if, we go public."

"Forget the 'if,' Danny. We must. We have no choice."

"But how, when, and with whom, Maya?"

Chapter Thirty-Five

A PLAN

"**W**hy don't you just give it in summary form to everyone, Danny, at exactly the same time, and see who bites? Post it from a random e-mail address, maybe even the *Spring Town Gazette,* sign false names, explain how we came to have all of the supporting documentation, snippets of which will be attached to the summary expose, promise the original documents to whatever legitimate organization or organizations want to take it on. Distribute it to every major news agency—print, broadcast, cable, online news agencies—again, simultaneously, and ask for a private-line telephone contact number, name, and title for follow-up. Then, simply wait out here in the deep woods for e-mail responses. If there are none, we sit on it all, and know that at least the curtain will have been lifted. If there are some, we decide which ones seem legitimate, which ones might be fronts for the bad guys to use to find us, and which ones, if any, warrant a follow-up phone call. Our decision only. There are significant risks involved, but any approach will bear some. This one, if we're lucky, will appeal to the competitive nature of breaking news journalists hungry for Pulitzer Prizes and the like."

All looked at Sammy in stunned silence. He had actually come up with a plan, an approach that seemed to make sense on the surface. Maya liked it for its simplicity and its distance from the Free People she was sworn to protect. Danny liked it for its broad reach, its anonymity, and its multimedia potential for generating a feeding frenzy. He knew all about that and had been part of it all of his career. Lynda like it because it hooked in a local media site owned by a local bad guy. Penny like it because it was Sammy's idea.

"Okay, does anyone have a better idea?" asked Maya.

There was no response.

"Can someone figure out how to access *a Spring Town Gazette* e-mail account?"

Penny nodded. "I believe that I still have my STG account unless they have shut me out. Let me check." Penny pulled out her iPad and punched the "new message" icon. She smiled.

"Still on board! They will see my name but I don't give a—"

"I do, hon," interrupted Sammy. "The bastards will try to kill you. Just like they did Richard and I'm sure countless others."

"At least they will know that I am alive and still kickin'. I can't believe they haven't cut off my access. This is a mistake I want them to pay for, particularly that fat-assed sheriff. I'll drive into town to send so they can't track us."

Sammy could only shrug then smile. "Whatever you want, Penny. Whatever you want."

"So, when do we launch?" asked Maya. "Are you ready to go, Danny?"

"Yes, just some summarizing and formatting issues, which won't take long. How about day after tomorrow?"

Chapter Thirty-Six

A STRINGER

Dutch Tippler is a stringer for a Midwestern independent newspaper, the latter a rarity in an industry that had collapsed upon itself amidst mergers and corporate buyouts. The *Daily Half Dozen* had carved out a niche market for itself by tackling controversial local and regional issues, reporting all sides of the debate, then taking a firm position, regardless of who may be offended. "Independent" was their watch word and their masthead spoke to the owners' desire to present six separate stories each morning, no more, no less, with a formal editorial page position on the one deemed most contentious. There were no obits, no restaurant inspection reports, none of the pap that the competition dwelt on. It was a format that had attracted a small but loyal following. Subscription revenues, supplemented by a few ads, were adequate to keep the presses running.

Dutch had once been more than a stringer. He had been a go-to reporter for a major national newspaper until his drinking got in the way. He still drank and now was paid by the piece rather than salaried.

The *Daily Half Dozen* was owned by the Robbernet family and managed by the matriarch, Dorothy, the aging but feisty widow of the founder. She personally selected each day's half dozen stories and wrote the editorial in support of the newspaper's positioning on one. Dorothy was particularly fond of Dutch's work. Not enough to hire him full-time because his drinking sometimes impaired his work ethic and adherence to deadlines. She simply admired his product and believed in his self-professed cardinal rule of never writing when drinking. And it was Dutch Tippler whom she called immediately when the e-mail from some Penny Plum at the *Spring Town Gazette* in Spring Town, Missouri, hit her desk.

"Dutch, can you come to my office immediately? I don't usually follow up on stuff like I just received but must admit after skimming through it and several attachments, I am stunned at the potential enormity of this story. I want to turn it over to you for a more thorough investigation and recommendation as to whether to take it seriously or not."

Dutch was a touch hungover but could sense the excitement in his boss's delivery. "I'll be there within the hour, Mrs. Robbernet."

—◆—

The more Dutch Tippler read, the more he drank. Vodka on the rocks with a twist.

Mrs. Robbernet had handed him a long e-mail with several attachments printed out and asked him to take a look. She was flabbergasted at the implications of any of it, if true, and needed an objective analysis before deciding whether to follow up as instructed. She had said little else.

It hadn't taken Dutch long to understand the gravity of the accusations included therein. A multinational, multi-agricultural conglomerate, multicurrency conspiracy to control global meat production, processing, and marketing, bypassing standard trading practices and treaties, laundering huge sums of money, and controlling critical production locales with bribery and extortion. Dutch couldn't even think in terms that large, let alone discern whether it could be possible.

The explosive e-mail had been sent from a newspaper in Spring Town, Missouri, presumably by a disgruntled employee with an endgame of who knew what. That's how far three drinks had gotten him. He was feeling slurred and disoriented and thought he might just lie down for a while. He had until 10 a.m. the following morning to report back to Mrs. Robbernet.

In other newsrooms and broadcast booths around the country, first reactions were muted. Some large news agencies dismissed the accusations as sophomoric, a rambunctious attempt at juvenile humor. Others laughed out loud at what they saw as someone's attempt to gain attention for their first pulp fiction novel. Still others just shrugged at more fake news and trashed the whole piece.

The competitive lust Sammy and Danny had hoped to stir up was buried in a surge of ridicule.

And the simple fact remained—the world of media was generally corporate-controlled. Big Ag and Big News had a lot in common, not the least of which was to protect the status quo and produce big profits. And, in a sense, each other. This was the way of the world these days, and breaking ranks over crackpot accusations and half-truths served neither "Big" well. "Why bother?" was the generally accepted response.

There were a few who took notice and submitted their private-line contact information to see what kind of response might be forthcoming.

One of those was Avarice Archibald at the *Spring Town Gazette*. He couldn't believe his eyes when the e-mail from his very own office under the name of Penny Plum was slapped on his desk by an assistant. He screamed for her to fetch Sheriff Slack and Deacon Duncan to his office as soon as humanly possible and then began to read. Each sentence elicited a new cringe. It was all so accurate, word for word. "Holy shit," he kept muttering and muttering to himself line by line. He was awakened from this bad dream by the sudden realization that no one had never shut down Plum's office e-mail and demanded that his assistant do so as soon as possible. He also asked her to hold all calls, as the phone began to ring incessantly.

Deacon Duncan was the first to walk into a cesspool of curses and rants. Sheriff Silas was not far behind.

"I'm afraid we've lost, gentlemen. Plumb has leaked a summary of our top secret documentation to press outlets around the country and offered to back the accusations included therein with solid evidence through secret channels. She even had the brazen nerve to send it out on her *Spring Town Gazette* e-mail, essentially from this office, from us. How could you have not eliminated her access to company e-mail in your rush to arrest her? It's your paper, Deak. It was your crime scene, Sheriff. How could you not have closed that window of vulnerability?"

Deak and the sheriff stared blankly at each other.

"The assistant secretary has already called me twice on my cell, and I've got to have some answers before I call him back."

"What if we followed the instructions for follow-up in the e-mail and provide a private telephone line number and contact information while indicating strong interest? What if we can trace our way back to Plum by posing as independent journalists wanting to cooperate with her in revealing the conspiracy?"

"Interesting, Deak. We'll need the phone number to be from an area code that she won't recognize. Do you know anyone in another news organization far away from here that we can trust without fail who could front for us? If we can just follow the thread to Plum, eliminate her, and reclaim our docs, we could still minimize the damage. We just need to control the evidence."

"I have a dear friend in Dallas, Texas, I can call. She's a news anchor for a local TV station. I think she might be willing to help."

"How do you know her, Deak?" asked Archibald.

"That's personal, Av. Let's just say that we have stayed very close over the years."

"Does she know about the Coalition, Deak?"

"Only in very general terms. And she is extremely trustworthy, Av."

"OK, give her a call and see if she will front for us. If so, I think you should head straight to Dallas and manage our inquiry personally."

"I'll make up something to tell my wife and be down there tomorrow morning, Av."

"I'll advise the assistant secretary's office of our plan and try to convince him that we are useful enough to keep around for a bit. Remember, Deak, our aim is to follow up with Plum as if we wish to publish this shocking information but to do so we need to see the evidence, personally. We are prepared to meet her anywhere as soon as possible to move things along. We also have to hope that most of the media world will think this so outlandish, so bizarre, so convoluted and fake that they won't follow up at all. We've got to move quickly, gents."

"What do you want me to do, Av?" asked the sheriff.

"Well, Sheriff, unless you have an old lover like Deak, one who might help us gain access to Penny Plum and her stash of documents, I think that I would start learning Mandarin Chinese."

—⁑—

Dutch Tippler knocked on Dorothy Robbernet's door at precisely 10 a.m. the next morning. She motioned for him to enter and sit down. His eyes were bloodshot and his clothes ruffled. Dorothy Robbernet sat quietly waiting for him to find himself. He had obviously thrown a big one the night before. What he said kind of surprised her.

"Mrs. Robbernet, I believe there is something here. It is so outlandish, so preposterous, so potentially enormous in scope that none of my journalist friends I have called this morning are paying much attention to it. While I respect, and in some ways agree with them, it is for that very reason I think we should move aggressively to take it on. A small, independent Midwestern newspaper can investigate a story like this without getting any flack from corporate or advertisers. And if it indeed becomes a story we can break, you will not be a small Midwestern newspaper anymore. I think we should go after it and am prepared to be point if you will allow me?"

"What about the drinking, Dutch? You know I don't hold that against you, and the magnitude of this story obviously did not inhibit your imbibing last night."

"You just have to trust me on that, Mrs. Robbernet. This may be a total bust and waste of time. So might I. Or it could be the scoop of a lifetime. I am willing to take that gamble. With your permission, I will respond to the e-mail as instructed, utilizing your personal line and our respective names and titles to try and arrange a meeting."

"Go for it, Dutch. It's all on you."

Chapter Thirty-Seven

BAIT AND SWITCH

"**D**anny, have you ever heard of the *Daily Half Dozen* before? Or Mrs. Dorothy Robbernet? Or a reporter named Dutch Tippler?" asked Penny.

"I've heard of the paper. It's kind of quirky in terms of format but has a very loyal following, mostly Midwest, but some national because of its approach to analyzing issues."

Penny and Danny were gathered around Maya's fireplace with her, beginning to process responses to their mass dump of incendiary information. There weren't many, to Danny's surprise. Not one major news organization inquired. There were a couple of "Are you kidding me?" and "Is this a bad joke?" but not much more. All Danny could conclude was that the story was too bizarre, too outrageous, too off-the-wall to attract serious attention from most newsrooms. This disappointed him because he felt he had laid out the case efficiently and effectively.

"Why do you ask about the *Daily Half Dozen,* and the names you mentioned?"

"Because they just responded. And then there is this inquiry from a Dallas television station, some reporter wanting to do a live interview with Penny and demanding a quick response. They won't touch the story without the interview. There are a few other indications of interest but not much more."

A piercing scream broke through the room. It came from Maya's bathroom where Lynda had retreated to sit in a tub of heated water, her weekly bath. All rushed in to find her sobbing, holding her ankle with one hand and swinging at a snake swimming in circles around her feet. It was truly a bizarre scene. A naked young lady and a terrified snake striking at her every kick.

"It's a copperhead," muttered Maya, grabbing the snake by the tail and smashing its head against the wall. "It must have come in through the drain. I've had that happen in winter before. Cold outside, seeking warmth, shedding hibernation for a moment of relative comfort, punching through the fragile stopper. She's been bitten." Maya wrapped a towel around Lynda and led her to the fire. "Let me see, Lynda."

"Heat some water over the fire," Maya commanded with calm authority. "I find at least three puncture wounds. A copperhead bite is rarely dangerous unless the victim descends into shock and stops breathing."

"Lynda." Danny sobbed. "Lynda, are you OK?"

Deacon Duncan and his female friend sat huddled around the secure phone in the TV studio's backroom. They had responded to the e-mail as instructed and were now just waiting, hopeful of a response. The call-tracking feature on the phone was activated and could pinpoint the location of any incoming call by satellite. There had been very little chatter around the media circuit, so Deak was guessing the lack of attention might give them a shot at a telephone interview. The sheriff was on alert to follow up with any positive location ID in the Ozarks, where all assumed the documents were stashed.

"How long are you going to wait, Deak, my love?"

"At least a couple of days if you think you can make it worth my while. Like pick up where we left off last night?"

Maya cleaned the copperhead bites with soap and warm water, but they were already beginning to swell.

"Maya," Danny cried, "Lynda's eyes are rolling up into her head, and she is barely breathing. What can we do?"

Maya reached slowly under her tunic and pulled out a leather pouch attached to a cord around her neck. She opened the pouch and took a pinch of pink powder from it. She tilted Lynda's head back to open her mouth and placed the powder under her tongue. Every movement was very slow and measured.

Thirty seconds passed and then a minute. Lynda's breathing became deeper and more regular.

Suddenly she sat up with a start, drooling slightly from her mouth but clearly back in control of her reflexes. Danny hugged her with a sob and then hugged Maya. Penny looked at Sammy and turned to Maya.

"That was amazing, Maya. What was the pink powder that reclaimed her senses and returned breathing to normal?"

"Just an old family recipe, Penny. It can cure about any ill."

"I'm not sure what we just witnessed," Sammy whispered to Penny after Maya left the room to go clean the mess in the bathroom. "But it bordered on miracle. I was convinced we were going to lose her when she began convulsing and then Maya and her magic potent. What is it with this lady? She is truly different."

"I sense the same, Sammy."

—ʍ—

"Well, we've cast our bait far and wide and have little to show for it," Danny noted as calm returned to the cabin deep in the woods. The few telephone interview requests, including the one from a major station in Dallas. spook me a little. Modern technology can pinpoint our location and lead anybody, good or bad, to us. I didn't like the pushy feel of the Dallas request either. I say disregard all of them and focus on a couple of the journalists who responded. Broadcast news was probably a bad idea to begin with."

"That's not a large pool to pull from either," noted Penny. "And not a single major newspaper even gave us the dignity of a serious response."

"Agreed, but one in particular kind of intrigues me. I told you that I have heard of the *Daily Half Dozen*. It is a real live newspaper with a format and following, which lends itself to this kind of story. I checked online and the Robbernet family owns the paper, Dorothy Robbernet is listed as publisher and editor, and though I had to dig around a bit, I finally found something on a journalist named Dutch Tippler. He was a star reporter for the *Chicago Tribune* at one time but simply dropped out of view. Nothing on the net as to why. He is listed as a 'stringer' for the DHD, which means paid by the piece. So, an actual—albeit regional—newspaper, a publisher/editor, and a reporter formerly held in high regard at a national newspaper. All the makings of a partnership to get this story out."

"I'm intrigued, too," added Maya, "but how does a paper that commits to six major stories a day handle a multifaceted bombshell like we are providing?"

"Good question, Maya, but if you stop and think about it, there are six big headlines and six riveting bylines in just about every aspect of this insidious multitentacled plot. Here is what I suggest. We have a product, condensed into a manageable narrative, and backed with reams of corroborating documentation. We have very limited interest in following up on such a vacuous and neverending story. We can't use broadcast media because of the risk on-air interviews subject our hidden location to. We have one reasonably credible bite, the *Daily Half Dozen*. Penny will respond to their indication of interest. I will fly to meet the publisher/editor and reporter and, if satisfied with their legitimacy, will submit to a formal interview and provide them with our summary documents to study while I further organize the treasure trove of evidence. They will sign a formal confidentiality agreement which outlines the conditions under which they may go public with the whole story, including the staging and timing of release."

"We can't let you do this, Danny. It's too dangerous," whined Lynda.

"Not as dangerous as doing nothing. As Maya pointed out not long ago, 'if' we release is not an option. It is only 'when' and 'how.' The only way this multinational nightmare can end is if we reveal the breadth and depth of its corrupt reach. No one can do it except us. And no one even knows who I am. No one is looking for me. No one wants to kill me. I don't even live here."

"Danny is correct," spoke Maya softly. "And I agree with his plan, with a couple of tweaks. Penny, please respond to the request received from the *Daily Half Dozen*, agreeing to an initial interview in a neutral location, say the Ritz in Clayco, Missouri. They can select the date. I will go with Danny, a talisman of good luck, if you will. No one is looking for me, either. Do not give them our names or contact information, noting merely that we will contact them in Clayco, once provided the details of their stay. The rest of you will remain here in the woods as our communications checkpoint."

Penny's head was spinning off her neck. What had begun as a Posse adventure in resistance messaging at a pig CAFO had become a full-throated attempt to bring down the beast itself.

Dutch Tippler looked in disbelief at the e-mail Mrs. Robbernet had thrust in front of him. It was short and to the point. "You sure you want to invest Ritz-sized dollars in me, Mrs. Robbernet? Two nights will cost more than you pay me for ten stories."

"As I said before, Dutch, it is all on you. I trust your judgement and instincts on a potential blockbuster story like this. Don't hesitate to walk away if something smells funny. Likewise, don't hesitate to commit us all the way if this is the real deal."

Chapter Thirty-Eight

A MEETING

The knock on the door was greeted by a tired-looking, middle-aged man, twitching with nervousness.

"Dutch Tippler?" the young man asked. He was accompanied by a strange, ageless-looking lady with an air of mystery shrouding her.

"Yes. And who are you, both of you?"

"That's not important, Dutch, but why we are here is."

Three hours later Danny and Maya exited, leaving Danny's summary expose, carrying an executed confidentiality agreement, and promising to return the next day with supporting documentation. They were committed to remaining in the hotel for as long as it took Dutch to digest what was being thrown at him and answer any questions they could. So many were unanswerable, they pointed out.

Dutch was on the phone with his publisher/editor after skimming through Danny's outline, which was frighteningly consistent with what he had listened to, albeit secondhand-sourced, from Danny and Maya.

"I think it's the real deal, Mrs. Robbernet. Getting my arms around it all will be the challenge. The conspiracy is colossal, the cover-up monumental. Even the backstory, of how this ragtag gang of resistors got involved, how they obtained the information, how they escaped the corrupt authorities trying to eliminate them, how they pulled it all together into a cohesive summary, is a compelling series in itself. It reads like a first-class spy story. And where they are now, hidden in the backwoods of a national forest in the heart of the Ozarks? What more can I say?'

"Are you sure it's not just that, Dutch, a first-class spy story, a novel, an entertaining piece of fiction?"

"No, not yet. But I will be. And I am going to need help. I need access to experts in international markets and trade, who can help me piece together how it all works, how the money flows, how the rules and the regulators are bypassed, and who are not involved in the con.

"That could be a pretty small universe, Dutch."

"I'm also going to need some financial whiz kids to help me understand and unpack the numbers in multiple currencies and denominations."

"I believe we can access such expertise on short notice, Dutch."

"The thing that blows my mind is the simple context of the whole scheme. It's not like someone or some group is trying to take over or rule the world. Just thoroughly control a unique niche and create great wealth for a few doing so. Three sovereign governments— or parts thereof, four corporate agriculture behemoths, operating clandestinely below internal controls and oversight. A secret multinational state of its own making, doing its own bidding, feasting at a trough of arrogance and greed, imbibing a heady elixir of power and privilege, all in the name of personal enrichment. Environmental and quality-of-life considerations be damned."

"Write that down before you lose it, Dutch. That alone will sell papers, and we might even be able to bring down the whole mess along the way. Do some good for humanity and the environment and educate the general public to the dangers of concentrations of power, the need for regulation, checks and balances, the value of a free and unfettered press.

"Write that down, too, Mrs. Robbernet."

"I'm also going to need to spend more nights at the Ritz. My sources have promised to return tomorrow with a treasure trove of documentation to share, as long as I'm on board with the general theme. And we haven't even gotten to how to rollout and maintain continuity of message. Or assuring the personal safety of all involved. I executed a formal confidentiality agreement to that effect this morning."

"Excellent. The checkbook is open, Dutch. And as soon as you can assure me that this is not a hoax about another hoax, you have full authority to carry this one to the finish line. And please call me Dorothy and lose the Mrs. Robbernet. We are going to be very close by the time this is over, Dutch."

"Yes, ma'am. Dorothy."

Chapter Thirty-Nine

DISAPPEARED

Sheriff Silas Slack and Deacon Duncan simply disappeared. Whoosh. Gone. Overnight. Their families felt, or feigned, grief at their loss but could offer no rational reason or explanation.

For Sheriff Silas, it had been as he left the office to enter his squad car for home. A black Lincoln Continental screeched up beside him, and two heavyset hooded men pulled him into the back seat. He was never seen again nor was his body ever found. His chief deputy took over the department until the next election cycle. His first case was to figure out what happened to his former boss.

Deak was nabbed as he left the airport after returning from his successful little love-in and failed effort in Dallas to connect with the suspects. He had flagged down a cab, which wasn't a real cab, to take him home. He was never seen or heard of again, either.

The entire original Spring Town regional leadership triumvirate was gone: Editor Bottoms, Sheriff Slack, and Deacon Duncan. As were the documents they were sworn to secure and protect. They had represented no more than an unacceptable risk to higher-ups at the end, so they were disappeared. Only Avarice Archibald remained and that only by the grace of the assistant secretary himself. Threatened initially with recall to Washington, Avarice begged to remain, promising to flood the community with good news and happy pictures rather than simply shut the *Spring Town Gazette* down, leaving a void for alternative truths to circulate and fester. He felt that he could negotiate a reasonable arrangement with Deacon Duncan's widow, who now was listed as owner. He had in fact struck up a relationship with her during the time Duncan had been missing, which he might be able to leverage into something more, even a controlling interest. There apparently had been no love lost between her and her cheating husband.

Amidst the coming of spring, all of Spring Town was abuzz about all that was going down.

—∿—

Dutch Tippler spent the two days after receiving supporting evidence of an unprecedented global conspiracy in total seclusion. He had not one drop of vodka nor any alcohol for that matter. He ate little and lived on coffee. It reminded him of his days as an ace reporter for the *Tribune*, though he had never covered a story like this one in his entire career. He was convinced that Danny and Maya were telling the truth, and it was his job to package and message that truth into a full public service disclosure.

Danny and Maya remained on call 24/7 and responded several times to Dutch's questions, declining only when the privacy of the Free People was put on the table. Dutch really wanted to talk to Penny firsthand to learn more about her harrowing journey from Posse duty, to wounding, to hounding by the sheriff and his henchmen, to discovery of the treasure trove of incriminating documents, to escape under the cover of night, to hideout in the Ozarks woods. As Dutch laid out a series of story releases in his mind, focusing on maximum audience exposure and minimum risk to all involved, he kept coming back to Penny and Sammy to set the stage for plot exposure and humanize the context of storytelling.

Danny and Maya reluctantly agreed to drive back to fetch Penny and Sammy and return to the Ritz for personal interviews. They were extremely concerned about the two leaving their safe cocoon in the forest but understood Dutch's rationale.

—∿—

Penny Plum and Lynda Leopold sat hugging then shaking upon hearing the news of Sheriff Slack's and Deacon Duncan's

disappearance and the high likelihood of foul play. Good rid-
dance was what first came to mind, then fear, sheer fear of the
ruthless unknowns who had so quickly and efficiently eliminated
their persecutors. Without a trace. At least the bastards would
never see Penny's bullet wound scar.

The ladies knew it had to have something to do with the pre-
liminary release of what all had come to call Posse Tracks. They
could only imagine the furor that would follow proper and wide-
spread publication of Danny's story. Heads would roll, and lives
would be lost.

Hopefully not theirs.

When Maya texted Dutch's request for an interview, Penny
and Sammy hesitantly agreed, and Lynda begged to go along.
She was afraid to be anywhere alone. Maya and Danny would be
there to fetch them within twelve hours.

Penny didn't like the idea of the five principal witnesses in this
earth-shattering matter going anywhere together, particularly
the shadowy, cruel, outside world that awaited.

Chapter Forty

TRANCED

When Danny saw the flashing red lights in his rearview mirror, a quick glance at his pedometer revealed the reason. 80 mph in a 65-mph zone. "Shit," he cursed and began to pull over. It was late at night, and it was several minutes after he stopped that a tall, slender deputy sheriff strode up and motioned for him to roll down his window.

"License and registration, please."

Danny complied as the officer shined his flashlight on the other faces in the car, Lynda up front, Maya closest to him in the back seat, Penny and Sammy huddled together in the far back corner.

"Now I need to see all of your licenses, please."

"Why?" asked Danny.

"That is none of your concern, sonny. Now let me see them." Each in turn passed them to the officer. He studied each one carefully before pulling one out and shining his light on Penny, studying her face carefully. Then Sammy next. "Step out please, both of you, and walk around to me slowly, very slowly."

They did as ordered and stood at least a foot shorter than the deputy, who stared down on them, back and forth, and then caught Maya's intense gaze out of the corner of his eye.

"I'm afraid that I'm going to have to take you in, Ms. Plum and Mr. Spode," the deputy growled. "There is an APB out for you two in regard to the disappearance of Sheriff Silas Slack, Spring Town, Missouri."

The deputy's gaze was drawn back to that of Maya, who fixed her eyes on his with an intensity that almost sizzled. His face went blank, and he wobbled slightly before heading back to his vehicle.

"Get in quickly you two and get us going at the speed limit, Danny, to Clayco. The deputy will remember nothing, but we've got to get off the road if they are looking for Penny and Sammy. To disappear them as well, I'm guessing."

Penny and Sammy quickly reentered, but Danny couldn't move. He had seen it all. "What did you just do, Maya?"

"Let's just say I 'tranced' him, Danny, and that is all you need to know. And on second thought," Maya added, "Penny and Sammy, I want you to crawl in the trunk together for the short remainder of our journey. The forces arraigned against us are far more powerful and well-resourced than we can even imagine. And no messing around back there," she laughed. Penny and Sammy didn't ... laugh.

Twenty minutes later they were in Danny's and Maya's rooms respectively, mulling over Maya's admonition to say nothing to Dutch Tippler about what had transpired or she might have to "trance" them.

At this point no one wanted to mess with Maya.

Chapter Forty-One

THE BACK STORY

A ll gathered in Dutch's room, encircling Penny and Sammy. "I want to hear the backstory from you two, every memory, every detail. Leave nothing out. My job as a journalist is to synthesize what has happened in a compelling and factual manner that will stimulate the reader's interest and imagination. I want them to be you for a moment, to feel your fear and fury, to step out of their skins into yours. I intend to use the backstory to introduce the whole sordid affair if you choose to go forward with us. I will record your recollections if you don't object."

Penny and Sammy nodded concurrence.

The next two hours were filled with more twists and turns, ups and downs, raw excitement and twisted intrigue than Dutch could recall ever reporting on.

Avarice Archibald wasn't through just yet. While a draft of the Coalition's records had been dumped on journalistic and media outlets almost a week earlier, nothing else had surfaced since, leading him and his superiors to believe that it had all been too preposterous for even the most callous reporters to follow up. Fake news of the most ludicrous order. That said, he was still itching to get his hands on Penny Plum and Sammy Spode. He knew that the national organization was pursuing them regionally under the guise of foul play involving Sheriff Slack. And he was continuing to follow up on the leads generated by Slack and Duncan during their interrogations. Lynda Leopold had never been located, and he had brought in several of the assistant secretary's boys to apply pressure to anyone who knew her. He still continued to consider her a possible link to Plum and Spode, though he couldn't put his finger on it.

He had also recently learned more about a hippie commune out in the Mark Twain National Forest around the upper reaches of Goose Creek. Probably nothing there but a bunch of filthy dropouts and free lovers, but no official, even Sheriff Silas, had ever checked it out personally. Who were they and what were they dropping out from? He would send several of the assistant secretary's boys out there as well, just to look around.

—⁂—

"Maya."

"Yes, Darvin," Maya whispered into the phone to avoid distracting from the story unfolding on Dutch's bed.

"There's strange fellows about out here creeping around, asking questions, writing down names. No one's ever done this before. The threatened to bust me for my weed if I didn't tell them where Penny Plum and Sammy Spode are. Or even Lynda Leopold. Thankfully I don't even know who, let alone where, these folks are. But there is talk around that you might be housing some folks, and if it's them, I wanted to warn you."

"Thanks, Darvin. You are one of the chosen few who know how to contact me, and while I can assure you that no one by those names is around in the deep woods, it is important information. Please inform the others in your circle of our conversation and keep me posted on who and what is happening. My guess is that these are not good people and under no circumstances should anyone trust or confide in them anything about our lifestyle or beliefs. Is that clear, Darvin?"

"Yes, Maya. And' I will stay in touch."

—⁂—

"There's just not much out there. It's like you said, a bunch of ill-clothed, illiterate hayseeds, without much to say. They call themselves the 'Free People' or something like that. 'Free of what?' I asked one particularly stoned guy with his half naked wife or partner or girlfriend sprawled across his midsection. 'Of dudes like you,' he had responded with a goofy giggle. Spooked me."

"Very secretive, very uncouth. No whys, hows, numbers, names, or reasons. I even threatened to bust a couple of them for weed or indecent exposure but got nothing but shrugs in return. Like they could have cared less. Still, I think we need to keep an eye on them and stick our heads in every now and then to let them know we are watching."

These were the assessments of the assistant secretary's boys. Didn't sound much like a threat to Av, but he nodded his approval to periodic surveillance.

—⟋⟍—

When Penny and Sammy had finished their rapid-fire tell-all, Maya interrupted to advise that they would be staying at the Ritz for a while. The bad guys had made their way into the woods and among her people. They were looking for Penny, Sammy, and Lynda.

"We can't afford this place, Maya," Penny whined.

"Yes, you can," countered Dutch, tossing his credit card on the bed.

Just then, Maya had a provocative thought. She smiled softly at Lynda.

"Send your Posse out at 2 a.m. this morning on a mission. It's been a while since you've pinged them, and I think some messaging to this whole secret apparatus might be appropriate."

"Brilliant, Maya, brilliant," Lynda responded. Sammy and Penny could only smile at one another.

Later that early morning, PING.

Chapter Forty-Two

A POSSE, AGAIN

"They what?" demanded Avarice. The new acting county sheriff, Fennel Bard, was on the other end of the line.

"Someone or vigilante group or terrorist organization killed an even dozen head of livestock in CAFOs all over the Ozarks early this morning."

Av could only laugh at the absurdity of it all. "Killing pigs as an act of terror? You must be kidding. I remember Sheriff Silas and Deak talking about this at some point, but I figured that they were making it all up. This really happened, Fen?"

"Yes, Av."

"Wait a minute. This is what sheriff claimed led him to this Penny Plumb or whatever her last name is. She evidently was shooting Jimmy Johnson's pigs early one morning, and he got a bullet in her arm before she, or her sidekick, killed Jimmy. Wasn't that the story, Fen? This was way before she got her hands on—" Av stopped mid-sentence. Bard didn't know anything about the rest, the documents, the Coalition.

"What are you saying, Av?"

"Nothing, Fen, nothing. Listen. Do you think this could be related in any way to Plumb and her boyfriend? Some sort of messaging or such?"

"Don't have a clue, Av. I just know that there are hundreds of dead animals laying around and CAFO owners wanting to know what I'm going to do about it."

"What are you, Fen? What are you going to do? What did Sheriff Silas do when there was an outbreak like this in the past?"

"Nothing, Av, nothing"

"Speaking of which, have you come up with any leads as to where sheriff might have disappeared to? Or Deacon Duncan?"

"Nothing, Av, nothing. It's been more than a week since I bid the sheriff goodnight as he headed out to his squad car half a block away. He evidently never made it there. It was locked up tight with no sign of activity when we checked it out the next morning. The sheriff was never seen again as best we can determine. We have verified that Deak was on the plane as scheduled from Dallas, that he picked up his luggage and headed out to find a cab or ride, not sure of which. Never seen again, just like Sheriff Silas."

Avarice had to hide the smile that was forming on his lips. The assistant secretary's guys were good, really good. He could envision what happened to his former colleagues and was grateful that he was spared.

"So, what are you going to do about the animal assassinations, if that's what they are?"

"Nothing, I guess. Just like Sheriff Silas."

"Sounds okay to me. I'll keep it out of the paper. No need stirring folks up."

Chapter Forty-Three

ANTSY

They were all getting pretty antsy at the Ritz. Daily warm water showers, hot breakfasts, and morning papers were a welcome return to past normalcy. But they were on the cusp of paranormal at this point. For now, they couldn't go back to the woods, they couldn't leave the hotel, they couldn't speak to anyone beyond themselves with the exception of periodic communication between Maya and home base.

Sammy decided to break the stalemate. With Dutch's help everyone had their own room now.

He and Penny had just enjoyed intimacy for the first time in weeks, and both were full of joy.

"OK, Penny, I'm really serious now. I want you to marry me right here, right now, in this fancy hotel. You say you love me, you are carrying my baby, and we are surrounded by our best, perhaps only remaining, friends. Maya can surely handle the formalities, with all the wisdom and magic she lends to any situation. You say you want to get back to a normal life before adding permanence. I'm not sure our lives will ever be normal again. I want to take you out for days and nights at a time on Goose Creek, Penny. Make love on a gravel bar like we did that very first time. But when do you see that happening again with all the secret agents and hired guns prowling around the woods? When "Posse Tracks" goes live, our lives, apart and together, are put in even more perilous circumstance than even today. I want you, and I need to formalize what we both believe inside and know to be right. Marry me, Penny. I beg you on one knee," Sammy pleaded as he knelt naked in front of her.

"Put on your clothes and I'll give your proposal serious consideration." Penny laughed.

Twenty-four hours later, Penny and Sammy stood in front of Maya, who was outfitted in her beautiful loose sarong. Lynda flanked Penny, Danny stood next to an absurdly smiling Sammy.

They were situated in a small ballroom, which Dutch had procured for the ceremony. Dutch took pictures with his cell phone.

Maya spoke to them in mystical terms, invoking human and animal spirits from realms beyond. Dutch thought it had a touch of religion in it, but he couldn't be sure. When she finished, Maya pulled a tiny flute from beneath her dress and presented a haunting tune none had ever heard before. Dutch halfway expected the patterns in surrounding wallpaper to start spinning. She replaced the flute next to her body and motioned all to move closer toward her, placing arms around one another "in love," as she put it.

"With the powers granted me by the Free People and the ones who have gone before them, I pronounce you husband and wife, Sammy and Penny, and bless your union with love and happiness. You may kiss the bride, Sammy. ... You may stop now, Sammy"

Dutch reached toward the bottle of champagne chilling in a silver stand amidst the laughter. He popped the cork and poured, offering the first toast to "two brave souls who are risking everything to make the world better."

Glasses clinked, and Sammy pulled Penny close, patting her belly and taking away her champagne glass before she sipped.

"Don't want she or he to get drunk," he smiled.

Penny Plum and Sammy Spode had never been happier, despite the convoluted circumstances they found themselves in.

Chapter Forty-Four

'TILL DEATH DO US PART

The plain white manila envelope was slid beneath the suite room door while Sammy was showering, preparing for wedding night love with his new bride.

Penny had been asked to stay behind for a quick photo shoot with a hotel photographer wanting to use her to promote the Ritz Hotel Wedding Package. Sammy was aghast when Penny agreed and pulled her aside. "We're hiding out, hon, remember? There are bad guys all over world looking for you, and you're just saying here I am? Maya wouldn't like this."

"Look, Sammy, this is probably the most important day of my life and I have a professional photographer wanting to commemorate it. I asked when the promotion will begin and he indicated at least three months or so to coincide with the summer wedding season. No one knows we're here now, and we'll be long gone to somewhere else by then. Probably still in protective custody as "Posse Tracks" will be making history and bringing down thugs everywhere. Besides, it's me flipping my middle finger at all the bastards and saying F-U in a most civilized way. I want it, Sammy. I want a special memory of this day, this moment, and he will send it to me as soon as I can provide him a mailing address. I have his phone number right here and explained we will be traveling on our honeymoon and prefer for him to wait until we return. It will give me time to come up with a safe mailing address. And Dutch will be here with me all the time, getting his own shots. It's OK, Sammy, it's OK."

"I still don't like it." Sammy shrugged. "Just don't be long," he added before heading to the elevator and punching the top floor button. One of Penny's most endearing traits was her pluckiness, he laughed to himself. "F-U, huh? Ha!" Maya, Lynda, and Danny had already excused themselves in the spirit of privacy, Lynda and Danny hoping to find some of their own.

Sammy was surprised to find that Penny had not returned when he finished drying off. And even more confused as to why the envelope was there, addressed to him, Mr. Spode. Maybe the bill? But they weren't checking out yet? He opened it slowly, unfolding a letter-sized page with a typed note in bold caps. His confusion turned to terror.

"Dear Mr. Spode, we have your new wife Penny in our possession, and will *kill* her if the documents you and she illegally obtained are not returned to our possession within 24 hours, or if there is further mention of their contents in the public domain. There will be no further communication between us until sixty minutes before the aforementioned deadline. We are very serious. Just ask Sheriff Silas Slack or Deacon Duncan."

Chapter Forty-Five

MISSING

Dutch regained consciousness slowly. He found himself locked in a storage closet of some sort with barely enough room to unwrap his limbs. It had all happened so quickly and innocuously. He remembered Penny looking beautiful in her simple white dress that Maya had picked out and that he had procured for the wedding. He vaguely remembered the ceremony itself but was quickly fixated on the gentleman staging photos he claimed were for a Ritz wedding promotion. He seemed to know what he was doing, so Dutch simply followed him around, using the same angles as him to accentuate the beauty of the bride. And then all had gone dark, just after a sharp pain in the back of his head.

It was clear he had been attacked and imprisoned by someone who wanted Penny and knew what they were doing. He had to get out of this and find Penny. If it was the bad guys, they were all in trouble, as was his reporting to come. What do you mean "if?" he muttered to himself before pounding heavily on the closet door and screaming for help.

"We've got her, Av. We have Plumb."

"What? How? Where?" blubbered a delighted Avarice Archibald. "Who is this I am speaking to?"

"Name doesn't matter, but I work for the assistant secretary and have been part of a team focused on finding Plumb, Spode, and the documents for the past several weeks. Our efforts have been centered in the St. Louis area because of the significant local press presence and publication opportunities. We found them in Clayco, Missouri, a ritzy suburb to the west."

"For the record, her name is Plum, without the 'b,' not that it matters now that we have her. How did you pull it off, and is she still alive? Do you have Spode, as well, or any others they may have been traveling with? Do I know you? Have we worked together before? Is that how you know my nickname?"

"Yes, no, yes, yes, and yes, Av. But first things first. We stumbled onto Plum, and thanks for the correction, Av, pretty much through blind luck at the Ritz in Clayco, basically just making the rounds. An undercover team recognized her from the photos contained in our intelligence file just as she was walking through the lobby to a small side reception room to get married."

"To Spode, I presume?"

"Yep. The team concocted the idea of one of them posing as a professional photographer for the Ritz and talked her into hanging around after the ceremony for some promotional photos the hotel could later use to promote their wedding-friendly venues. She was reluctant at first, but they promised her that the rental fee for the room would be waived in exchange for a ten-minute session and that they would provide her with memorable photos from her special day. She bid the rest of her party a brief goodbye, with the exception of an older guy who was also taking pictures. We still don't know who he is, but while one of our operatives was snapping away with a proper camera he always carries, the other slipped behind and coldcocked the old guy, before stuffing him in storage closet. They did the old handkerchief-over-the-mouth deal to shut Plum down, checked into the hotel, and carried her up to a room for securing. Claimed she had celebrated her big event with a little too much champagne. All in all, a brilliant ad-lib if I have ever heard of one."

"Brilliant, indeed."

"A ransom note has already been delivered to the Spode kid, demanding the documents back and total silence going forward in exchange for her life. I've brought in two backup officers to keep watch over her for the next twenty-four hours, the deadline for the exchange we have set. I'm certain Spode will comply. Don't know who or where the rest of the wedding party is, but we'll find out."

"Well done, well done."

"Oh yes Av, the assistant secretary's office says you can do whatever you wish with her. We're obviously never going to give her back, and I know you have a special animosity toward her and Spode."

"Wow, what a gift! I do have some ideas as I believe she and Spode can lead us to a bigger pot with the right encouragement. There is this stealth group of resistors in the Ozarks who shoot CAFO livestock for no good reason, and I would like to put them out of business once and for all. I think Plum and Spode can help me crack the code."

"Do you want us to detain Spode?"

"Not just yet. But if you have enough manpower to put a tail on him it might help. I know he will beat it back here at some point, and I would just like to see where he lands. And if you can get some IDs on the rest of the wedding party, that will help as well. How are you going to handle the bogus transaction?"

"Well, we are going to leave another note for Spode, inviting him to come to a room at the Ritz exactly one hour before the deadline to drop the documents and reclaim Ms. Penny, I guess Mrs. Spode now.

"And then what are you going to do with her?"

"Like I said, whatever you wish. The assistant secretary's office has given you free rein. If you want her dead, we'll kill her. If you want her roughed up, we can do that."

"I've got to tell you, friend, whichever one you are, I am truly grateful for the assistant secretary's retention of trust in me again. I was worried after the bumbling fools let the docs and the thieves get away. He had threatened me with recall and reprograming in DC but has since entrusted me with responsibility. "

"You be the man for the Coalition in Missouri now, Av. I know he has been pleased with how you have handled the flow of information around the disappearance of Slack and Duncan, namely none, and your commitment to root out this clandestine resistance movement in Spring Town and surrounds. The full resources of his office are available if you can get your arms around it all. It needs to be eliminated, along with those who conspire against our program. He obviously feels you are capable of leading that effort. We need more CAFOs in the Ozarks, more protein to ship around the world, more profits. Not less."

"That's my job, friend."

"And about Mrs. Spode, Av?"

"I think I want you to ship her down her as soon as possible. I've got another bumbling sheriff who can lock her up and hopefully draw her kind out in the open to try and save her. And what are you going to do if they don't produce our files?"

"Kill them, I guess. But I'm not worried about that. They will come for the bride, and when she's not here, we send them on a wild goose chase to where we claim she will be. Sooner or later they will beat tail back home to you and whatever entrapment schemes you can conjure up. Will try to find out more about the rest of the party and get back to you. Consider Penny Plum Spode on the way home to handle as you wish."

Chapter Forty-Six
A BLUFF

Maya took control as soon as Sammy called her in a panic about Penny's abduction and the ransom note. "We must not be seen with each other. We are all in as much danger as Penny, as well as all of those around us, including the entire nation of Free People. I'm renting a car immediately to return to them. I'm taking Lynda and Danny with me. Not sure they know who we are yet, or they would probably have moved on us. No one must contact me or us. Sorry to say, but I have greater responsibilities than just to you all. I will be in touch with you, not the other way around. Where is Dutch?"

"Don't know. Dead for all I know."

"Try to find him and figure out how to handle the demand for documents. I hate to be so blunt, Sammy, but there is no way that they are going to give Penny back to you. We are going to have to take her. I don't know how they could have found her or us in the first place, but they did, and they are now in control of our respective destinies, including our efforts to expose the conspiracy. My initial reaction is that you should hold back some of the most damning docs. They surely can't have a detailed inventory. That would allow Dutch to break the story and provide at least few pieces to authenticate it."

"What if they find out and kill Penny."

"Honestly, I think that they think she is more important to them alive than dead. At least that is my hope. They have probably already shipped her off somewhere."

"Hold on, Maya, someone is knocking at the door."

"Don't open without an ID, Sammy."

"It's Dutch, and he has an open wound on the back of his head. Are you OK, Dutch?"

"I am, but what the hell is going on?"

"Goodbye, Sammy. Danny will drop off his keys to you before we leave. Explain it all to Dutch and figure out a sane response, based on the assumption that you will not get Penny back tomorrow or anytime soon."

Sammy sobbed and slumped to the bed. After fifteen minutes he was able to regain some semblance of composure. At least enough to walk through the ransom demand, Maya's conclusion that under no circumstance would Penny be returned, and a review of alternative responses with Dutch.

"Maya is right, Sammy. Penny is no more than bait in this charade, and she does them no good if she's dead. We simply can't give those files back to the bad guys, Sammy. They are the only insurance policy we have to protect Penny and us."

Sammy pounded the coffee table and spurted tears. "You all just don't give a shit about Penny."

"We do, Sammy, which is why we need to protect her by hanging on to the only thing that matters to these bastards. Hard evidence of their corrupt conspiracy to defraud humanity."

"So, what do we do, Dutch?"

"We slip out of here, get in Danny's car, and drive to your hideout in the woods where I can complete my full expose and put it and supporting documentation in the hands of my publisher/editor to release to the world. We need to go now and cover our tracks carefully. They obviously know who you are and will probably put a tail on you. We've got to beat it or lose it."

"You just want to make money and be famous again, Dutch," Sammy spat out.

"Do you have a better plan, Sammy? Or would you rather just show up at the appointed place and hour, be murdered or disposed of some other way, along with Penny, and let them destroy all of the evidence?"

Less than an hour later they were in the car, headed back to the Mark Twain National Forest, amidst the uncertainty of Penny's fate. They were careful to confirm that no one was following them.

—⚍—

"Spode hasn't responded to the note we slipped under his door, boss. I tried to call his room and no answer there either. There's no way they would run off and leave that little lassie to a fate worse than death is there?"

"Who knows? The girl is worthless without the papers, and besides, she has already been returned to Spring Town. Which is probably good. She's the only thing we have that might draw a response from these folks. I really didn't want to slit her pretty little throat, anyway. I'll let Av know that the whole party seems to have sprung the coop and are probably headed back to the Ozarks. I want you to gather several of your colleagues and head that way as well. Av can probably use the help. Don't suppose you got a tail on them."

"No, too late with coverage."

"These Spring Town hillbillies are either really smart or really good bluffers."

Chapter Forty-Seven

HOME AGAIN

"**G**ood evening, Ms. Plum. Or I guess it is Mrs. Spode now?" Penny could only stare at Avarice Archibald with disgust and disbelief, venom venting from her eyes. "What do you want, Avarice?"

"Please call me Av, like, you know, Ms. Plumb without the 'b.' Gets kind of irritating after a while, doesn't it? I want the documents you and you husband stole. You won't believe what has happened in Clayco. Evidently your new husband and wedding party don't think much of you. They stood up my colleagues who had arranged a swap deal, you for the docs."

"Seems to me they were pretty smart, Av. Kind of hard to close a swap when half the package has been hustled out of town."

"They would have killed you, Mrs. Spode, even with the handover of documents. I saved your life by bringing you home. At least for now. Nothing is sure if you choose not to cooperate. I need those files, the write-ups, the materials, the photos, and I need them now. And I also need to know that they will never see the light of day. Finally I need to know who was in your wedding party and where I might find them. I can only protect you, and them, so long, Mrs. Spode."

"Oh God, you're my savior now, Av? Give me a break, and leave me alone. I wouldn't help you open the door to this cell if you were setting me free. And I sure as hell am not going to help you and your fellow criminals get out of the mess you are in."

—⁂—

Maya, Lynda and Danny were shocked to see Sammy and Dutch pulling up to the cabin, headlights off, coasting quietly through the trees.

Maya spoke first once they were all gathered inside.

"Are you sure you weren't followed? Did you cover up the entrance to the track off the dirt road coming in? They know who you are, Sammy, and were probably set on taking care of you at the swap."

"Think we beat them out. We left well ahead of the deadline and saw no indication of any tailing. We even turned off on some back roads to see if there were followers. There were none."

"OK, here we are, all safe, all together. Except Penny. We don't know where she is or whether she is even alive, only that the Coalition for Prosperity got her. Here is what we do know. They have what we want: Penny. And we have what they want: a treasure trove of documentation, facts, and enough evidence to bring down a corrupt multinational conspiracy, which includes our own institutions of government. And that a simple swap of 'wants' can never work because we each don't trust the other, and each will have given up our only point of leverage to no advantage. The threat of killing Penny to stop publication is gone. The threat of not publishing if Penny is returned was bogus to begin. It is a giant circle of impotent *quid pro quos*. We also know that they are aware of the Free People and our heavily wooded paradise, that there are probably enemy agents descending on the Ozarks as we speak, that Dutch needs a little more time compiling his story line and assembling the facts that support it, and that we are all in deep trouble. It is only a matter of time before they descend on our community and destroy it and us, unless Dutch can get his story out to his superiors before things unwind. Again, this is what we know."

The ping of Maya's phone coincided with her last statement. She studied the text message carefully before sharing. "Penny is in Spring Town, incarcerated in the jail, and being charged with the murders of Sheriff Silas Slack and Deacon Duncan, though no bodies have been found nor any motives established. She is guarded by a cadre of outsiders, military types, heavily armed and snooping around every corner. This is what Lynda's friend Lydia is reporting."

"I'm going to get Penny," blurted out Sammy.

"Sammy, you surprise me from time to time. That's not a half-bad idea. Let's think it through," mused Maya.

Chapter Forty-Eight

ON THE OFFENSIVE

Avarice Archibald and Acting Sheriff Fennel Bard sat across from each other in the sheriff's office, strategizing about how they might use Penny Spode to draw out some of the local dissidents who kept assassinating CAFO livestock around the Ozarks, as well as others who were directing their illegal activities. And, of course, Sammy Spode, prime murder suspect along with Ms. Penny, in the deaths of Sheriff Slack and Deacon Duncan. "I'm desperate to get them all," Av muttered.

Avarice was also sitting on the bigger question of how to recover the stolen documents before they ended up in the media world. Having dodged the first releases as disjointed and lacking credibility didn't ease his anxiety that another, more focused attempt was looming. He didn't fear the corporate media as much as an independent, big and savvy enough to make a splash. And he certainly couldn't tell the sheriff about the bigger question, though the presence of more and strange security forces on the ground must have caught his attention. Maybe not. Fen clearly was not a deep thinker. Best focus on stopping the cruelty-to-animals contingent and see where it leads.

"We could try to strong-arm her a little, Av. Just some little stuff to warn of harsher treatment to come if she won't cooperate?"

"You can try, Fen, but she's a pretty tough little number."

—⋙—

"If we're going in to get Penny, the first thing we need is a diversion, something to pull all the goons away from the jail for at least a couple of hours," offered Maya. "Danny, I don't think any of them know you, correct? What if you go to the acting sheriff in the morning and advise that you have wind of an impending CAFO animal attack tomorrow night late? Take a map with targeted CAFO locations highlighted. I'm guessing you have one of those, Lynda, since you are the pinger-in-chief?"

"I do."

"I'm guessing they will be all over staging a preemptive raid on these renegades. Tell them they call themselves the Posse and that they are armed and dangerous. That staking out the sites early tomorrow evening will lead to mass arrests and incarcerations and put an end to their brutal malarkey. That you will even cover one of the sites yourself and bring a real live pig assassin to justice. When they ask how you know, you can answer, 'I just moved to town and have become buddies with one who is trying to recruit me to the gang. He's an organizer and even shared a map of targets to convince of the seriousness of their efforts after I played along.' You can tell them that you simply don't believe in what they are doing to innocent animals and want to stop it. If they don't bite, you will hightail it straight back to my cabin, and we'll come up with something different. If they do, you will likewise hightail it straight back and wait it out with Lynda and Sammy. I'll take care of setting Penny free and will need your car."

"I'm going with you to get Penny, Maya."

"No, you are not, Sammy. Everybody knows you, and we can't risk the exposure. You will stay here with Lynda, whom some know on sight as well, and Danny, and wait for our return. Meanwhile, Dutch, you will take everything you have for your first several days of columns, leading with the backstory of Penny and Sammy, and moving into vision, partners, financing, and operations, or however you told me you have it laid out, with supporting documentation. You will drive the rental car parked out back straight to your publisher/editor for her review and approval and get this expose going within the next forty-eight to seventy-two hours. You will be fine with the car because I rented it for a week, thinking we might need a getaway vehicle at some point. You can finish your entire body of work while the first segments are running."

"But, Maya, aren't you basically shutting down the Posse by giving away our name and game plan?" asked Sammy.

"Yes. The Posse has served its role with fervor and efficiency the past couple of years, but in two weeks we won't need it any more. A Coalition for Prosperity will be crumbling in its own multinational dust."

"I see," Sammy said with a smile. "I still wish you would let me go with you to Penny."

"No way, Sammy. None of this is without risk to you and to all of us, but Penny is worth it. This way we keep the known 'culprits'—you, Lynda, and, when freed, Penny—away from public exposure, and let Danny, Dutch, and me use our anonymity to pull it off. Danny, are you okay? You're going to the front lines."

"I'm just damn excited," shouted Danny.

"Is everyone in?" asked Maya with a hint of gravity in her voice. No one asked how she intended to free Penny, but all knew what sleight of hand, or mind, she was capable of.

"If not in, at least everybody's head is spinning," Dutch laughed. "I'll load up, be out of here in an hour, and drive all night. I've got enough on paper and enough documents to back it up to meet your deadline. I'm sure that my publisher/editor will 'be in,' as you put it, too."

Sammy shrugged reluctantly, and Lynda snuggled up next to Danny.

Chapter Forty-Nine
A LITTLE NIGHT MUSIC

S heriff Fennel Bard sat in stunned silence as Danny shared his story and map of targeted CAFO sites.

"I just thought you would want to know, Sheriff."

"Why are you doing this, son?"

"Because, friendship or not, I believe what they are doing to innocent animals is wrong, and I want to stop it.

"You know your friend will go to jail?"

"Yes. He's not that close, and what he is doing is wrong."

"How can I trust you, son?"

"Guess you will just have to, Sheriff. Besides, I intend to intervene at one of the sites myself and bring one of these assassins in to you to face justice for their cowardly acts. You may not have the manpower to cover the whole shooting range, but at least you can hit enough of them to send a serious message."

"I actually do have access to additional security officers who have been sent in from various posts around the state to look for this Plum Spode lady's accomplice in connection with the suspected murders of my predecessor, Sheriff Slack, and his business associate, Deacon Duncan. I think I can get command of them for an important operation like this."

"Seems strange that they would send in so many extra men just for a murder investigation."

"Yes, I don't really get it since we don't even know if murders have taken place. No bodies, no leads, really no links to much, but then again, I'm not privy to the whole game plan. I just report to Av Archibald, who seems to be directing it all. I will need to clear this with him. I do know he desperately wants to get these gang members—you called them the Posse, I think—in the worst way. Sit tight. He may want to meet with you himself."

Fifteen minutes later, Av walked into Sheriff Bard's office and sat down across from Danny. "Just who are you, son?"

"My name is Danny Dufford, and I'm a relative newcomer to town. I'm a journalist by trade but moved here because of a girl."

"Tell me again how you came to know about this so-called Posse group and get the target CAFO siting map."

Fifteen minutes later Avarice Archibald was on board. "I want to bring these criminals to justice, and we have the extra manpower to pull off a raid like this. Hell, Spode is probably one of them, and we might even get a 'twofer'! You say it's scheduled for midnight tonight, and we would need to have our agents in place no later than 9 p.m.?"

"Yes, sir."

"Well we can't cover them all but can sure send a message. Sheriff Bard, I want to leave at least two guards close to Ms. Spode's cell. We have her in solitary, and I just want to make sure she stays there. You are free to assign the rest a site on which to pay a preemptory visit. Two to each one, so there are no escapees. I want every one of these murdering Posse bastards under lock and key by eight tomorrow morning. I'll be here to greet them personally. You hang around late tonight to help check them in, Sheriff."

"Yes, sir, Av."

"Tell me again the name of your friend who is recruiting you so aggressively."

"I'd rather introduce him to you in person tomorrow morning, Mr. Archibald. Under lock and key, as you put it. I can handle him by myself."

"Look forward to the pleasure of making his acquaintance."

—⚇—

It was a little before 9 p.m. when Maya rang the doorbell at the sheriff's department. It took a while for Sheriff Bard to awaken from his doze and wander over from his office to open the door. "Please come in." He smiled at an unusual-looking lady, who promptly complied.

"You are working late, Sheriff Bard. Are you alone?" Maya asked. The sheriff appeared to be the only one around as Danny had promised. Maya scanned the premises then added, "It is important that I have a few minutes alone with you."

"I am the only one here at this time and to whom do I have the pleasure of speaking?"

"My name is Gracie, and I have been watching you from afar, Sheriff."

"Please come into my office and have a seat. May I help you with your coat?"

"Yes, Sheriff," Maya smiled as Sheriff Fen removed a jacket that left very little that remained to the imagination. Sheriff Bard could only stare. She shut the door to his office quietly, pushed the lock button, then sat, bare legs crossed across from his desk.

"Do you like what you see, Sheriff?"

"I would say so, ma'am."

"Would you like to see more?"

"I would, Ms. Grace, I surely would."

"As I said Sheriff Bard, you have been on my radar for some time. First, I love the sight of a fit man in a uniform, and you certain fill that profile well. Second, I work in the diner across the street and am afforded frequent views out of our front window of what I will call your sexy swagger, Sheriff. Confident, bold, upright, full of manhood. You don't visit us often, and I've never had an opportunity to personally wait on you, but you have certainly caught my attention. I am not usually this aggressive in pursuit of something I want, but when I got off work and walked by, I saw your light on. I followed my first impulse. 'Why not take a chance?' I asked myself. Are you married, Sheriff?"

"No, ma'am."

"Well neither am I," Maya added, as she slipped out of her see-through blouse. She wore nothing underneath. "Would you like a closer look, Sheriff Bard?"

The sheriff could only nod, without taking his eyes off Maya's bounty. Maya rose, slipped behind the sheriff's desk, and sat on his lap facing him. She placed his hands on her breasts and sighed deeply. When the sheriff was slow to respond, Maya stood and reached for his midsection.

"Why don't we take this big old gun belt off and see what lies beneath?" She unbuckled it and placed it on sheriff's desk

"Lean back and relax, handsome sheriff," she said, beginning to unbutton his pants and slide down his zipper. "Let's see what we have to work with." Sheriff did as told, shutting his eyes as she began to rub him.

The next thing the sheriff became aware of was staring into the barrel of his very own service revolver.

"Thanks for your cooperation, Sheriff Bard. You are going to help me free Ms. Penny Spode from incarceration or die not trying. Please dial up your jail supervisor and order him to bring her to your office immediately, that you have an important line of questioning to pursue with her in private that may involve some methodology that they probably don't want to involve themselves in. Do it now, Sheriff."

Fifteen minutes later, blouse firmly back in place, Maya held the gun to the back of sheriff's head as he cracked the door and ordered the two jailers to release Ms. Spode into his custody for the next couple of hours.

"We weren't told about this, Sheriff Bard, and it runs against regulations."

"Don't worry, I will take full responsibility. I just received important new information about her new husband Spode and need to process it with her in private. Now let her come in on her own and beat it. See you in two hours unless I call to say I need more time. Got to finish this before the troops in the field return."

The jailers shrugged at each other and returned to their van. Penny looked on in confusion before stepping through the door and hearing it close behind her. She looked at the sheriff and then Maya. Maya shushed her with a finger to her lips.

Fifteen minutes later, Maya and Penny were headed back to the forest in Danny's car, leaving Sheriff Fen Bard tied in his chair.

The frustrated first operatives returning from the bogus raid were treated to yet another surprise in an evening full of them. The tightly bound sheriff didn't have a stitch of clothing on.

Chapter Fifty

DEBRIEFED

Avarice Archibald was in a snit as he stormed into the sheriff's office at eight the next morning.

"You mean the whole raid thing was a shenanigan from start to finish? That you neither saw nor picked up a single member of that Posse or whatever they called it? That the instigator of this scam hasn't been seen since? That this was all one big distraction toward the goal of freeing Penny Plum Spode? And I reading you correctly?"

"Yes, sir," answered one of the men.

He then turned to Sheriff Bard. "You freaking idiot, Bard. The rest of you are dismissed. Sheriff, come with me into your office." His voice could be heard by everyone in the general vicinity behind the closed door.

"Tell me again what happened, Sheriff. You were seduced by a strange woman who took off her clothes to distract you. Enough so to steal your gun, hold you hostage, and coerce you into having Penny Plum Spode delivered with a bow on her head to her rescuer. Who was this lady?"

"Said her name was Gracie and that she worked in the diner across the street."

"Have you been over to see if there even is a Gracie that works there?

"No."

"And the two ladies stripped you naked and hog-tied you to the chair in your office? And you didn't even resist? You are the sorriest excuse for a law enforcement official I have ever encountered. Not only have you been conned in a flanking operation to free a critical suspect in multiple bad deeds, including murder, but you did it under the spell of sexual promise. You ought to be put in jail, Sheriff, without any clothes on, with a whole bunch of convicted sexual predators. That's exactly what I should do to you. Instead, you and I are going to cross over to the diner and see if there is even a Gracie on the payroll."

"Have a seat, gentlemen. As requested, your server Gracie will be with you shortly."

The men stared at each other, the sheriff with a glimmer of hope, until an elderly heavyset woman missing several teeth in her greeting smile said, "Morning, gentlemen, my name is Gracie."

Sheriff Fennel Bard dropped his head to the table and began to sob.

Avarice stood and stared down on his buddy Fen. "The past twelve hours have been nothing but one big f***ing distraction. And, we have lost our only bargaining chip along the way."

Less than an hour away, Sammy Spode held his new wife as tightly as he could to his naked body. He had doubted that could ever happen again.

Chapter Fifty-One

EXPOSED

Avarice Archibald's next day didn't get any better. In fact it became decidedly worse. A nightmare in the making.

It began with a phone call from the assistant secretary's office at about 6 a.m. It was the assistant secretary of agriculture for international affairs. The big boss man himself.

"Av, I don't know whether you've heard the news or read the big papers this morning, but the gig is up. Some midsize regional newspaper with a quirky name has released a bombshell summary of the Coalition's operational vision, goals, and leadership, complete with substantiating documentation, and promising more names, positions, and details. They even highlight Plum and Spode as heroes in the context of you and your bumbling idiots' efforts to catch them and suppress publication. The wire services have picked it up and it is spreading like wildfire. We can scream 'fake news' all we want, but unfortunately it is all basically factual. My name is already out there. Yours will be soon. I wanted to give you a heads up because of our long working relationship and your unfailing loyalty. But, Av, you are now on your own."

"What are you talking about, Mr. Assistant Secretary? On my own?"

"They, meaning the FBI most likely, will be coming for you very soon. One of our domestic corporate ag partners is whisking me off to a safe place hideaway, the location of which I am not even privy to, in exactly thirty minutes. I suggest you try and arrange a similar getaway with anybody or organization you have a personal connection with. You don't have much time, Av. Check out the *Daily Half Dozen* online, and you will understand our dilemma."

"Mr. Assistant Secretary—"
"Goodbye, Av. Godspeed."

—〰—

"They've done it," screamed Penny, awakening the whole brood of renegades squeezed into Maya's house.

They gathered around her computer and the *Daily Half Dozen* website.

"God bless you, Dutch Tippler."

The masthead read:

THE DAILY HALF DOZEN
OWNED, PUBLISHED, AND EDITED BY DOROTHY ROBBERNET
FOUNDED 1947
OMAHA, NEBRASKA

The day's lead headline: **DEEP AG, THE 51st STATE**
The daily half dozen topics from Dutch Tippler
The Coalition for Prosperity—Vision Statement

1) **"The Coalition for Prosperity envisions a world in which most are fed, a few get very wealthy, and we control the flow of goods and money."**

(continued on page 2)

2) **Signatories to the Coalition for Prosperity "Signatories include the respective Departments of Agriculture or their equivalents, from the countries of China, Brazil, and the United States of America, as well as four international agricultural conglomerates who control most meat production in the world."**

(continued on page 3)

3) **Operational Infrastructure**
"Delineation of operating responsibilities from the Assis-

tant Secretary, or Director, or Vice President of each of the seven signatories, down the chain of command to ground-level implementation, and including secret trading agreements, tariff exemptions, and payment mechanisms."

(continued on page 4)

4) Target Markets

"New lucrative target markets are identified and exploited for expansion of Confined Animal Feeding Operations (CAFOs)."

(continued on page 5)

5) Cash Flows, Following the Money, and Projected Impacts

"A giant circle of influence peddling, financial meddling, and corporate agriculture coddling is revealed in detail."

(continued on page 6)

6) Corruption, Bribery, and Sex

"A closed system for an inner circle of principally privileged men which exploits innocents around the world. Warning—details are graphic and unsuited for younger audiences."

(continued on page 7)

Each of these summary articles will be supplemented with substantiating documentation of a vast and illegal international agribusiness conspiracy over the coming days. See editorial page for commentary on two genuine heroes, Penny and Sammy Spode.

"Wow," was all Danny could think to say initially. "The *Daily Half Dozen* has dumped a half dozen blockbuster leads on an unsuspecting world." As a reporter and a journalist, he had never seen such a comprehensive expose of mass corruption presented so concisely and persuasively.

"Now, if we can just get the major news agencies and papers to shed their corporate logos for a while and start informing the public on critical issues again, the house of cards and CAFOs may fall forever."

But then, he continued, "Can you even imagine? We can take our meat supply, pricing, and availability back. We can take our state legislatures, county commissions, and city councils back. We can take government by and for the people back. We can break the backs of the price gougers and currency manipulators. We can encourage traditional family farming as a viable enterprise and begin a new run of multigenerational farmers and farmers' sons and daughters. We can take our land and our waters back, clean them up, and present them proudly to our children and grandchildren, and beyond. We can—"

"Slow down, Danny, and write it all down. I bet Dutch and his paper would run it as an op-ed," shouted Lynda to get his attention.

"I can't slow down, Lynda, I have hope to share."

Maya sat, smiling slightly. Penny clung to Sammy near the fire as he patted her baby bump.

"So, Maya, how far did you have to go with the bastard sheriff to bust him?" asked Penny.

Maya's smile broadened. "Not far, Penny, not far, and that is all I intend to share on the matter."

"Thank you all for risking so much to set me free. I apologize for my vain recklessness at the Ritz. I should have listened to Sammy ... but I was feeling so overjoyed ... and bulletproof. Guess I'll never get to see those wedding photos I almost died for."

"Don't worry, hon, I know Dutch got some. Besides we don't need them to preserve a moment we will share forever and beyond. It's seared into my heart and mind."

"What next, Maya?" asked Danny.

"I don't know, but we are not home free. None of us."

Chapter Fifty-Two

A PENNY FOR YOUR THOUGHTS

Penny could never get over how prescient Maya had always been. As she looked back over the past ten years she marveled that they had even made it. Sammy, then baby bump Nina and her younger brothers Sam, Jr. and Casey, Danny and Lynda and their children. It had taken years for them to even think in terms of "home free," and all knew that they were here today because of mystical, magical Maya.

They all hid out with Maya for close to two years as the world came unhinged, and then began to put itself back together again. They never learned what happened to people like Avarice Archibald and Sheriff Fennel Bard, but doubted they met happy endings.

Likewise, they were sure that not all the bad guys were brought to justice, but read about some pretty big heads rolling. The political fallout in their own country brought about changes in government at all levels. While the secretary of agriculture was never directly implicated, his deputy secretary for international affairs was and disappeared into a fog of never-ending rumors. Mr. Secretary himself was soon "retired."

The most damning aspect of the long subterranean charade was the widely accepted conclusion that departmental fractures throughout the United States government, from the FBI and CIA to Agriculture, to State, to Defense, to Commerce, and the Export-Import Bank, cast doubt on any consistent credibility in government messaging and claims to truth. That damage lingers yet today.

State and local governments were easier to clean up. Most legislators were guilty of some level of dollar-induced corruption.

Some went to jail, but most were simply thrown out by their constituents and replaced with more honorable representatives from a large pool of pissed-off citizens.

Corporate strongmen and their gargantuan bonuses took big hits, earnings tanked around the globe, stock values crashed, and recession stymied growth for most of the decade. The world was still in a very difficult recovery period.

Some pundits argued that we should have just let it be. Things were working fine, and jobs were plentiful. That crooked capitalism or bastardized oligarchism are more efficient than the free enterprise system. That "regulated free markets" is an oxymoron, not a viable alternative. Most did not buy such self-serving rationalizations.

There were threats against the Free People from unknown sources and for reasons even less obvious. Penny often wondered if they had to do with the rumored freeloaders that Maya was sheltering, that somehow word circulated among the tribe that they were with her, putting the clan's whole way of life at risk. She guessed that she would never know.

When the whole thing blew apart and visiting law enforcement retreated home, the surveillance and periodic encroachments ended. On several prior occasions Free People were threatened and even beaten, but none spoke their secrets.

And through it all, Maya kept her flock together and safe, despite the intrusions, nourishing, guiding, and encouraging all through treacherous times. Penny never did understand how she protected the location of her cabin. To be sure, it was buried deep in a darkest corner of the Mark Twain National Forest. There were only a very few of her trusted lieutenants who knew where and not one of them ever visited. Thankfully her secrecy provided a veil of security for all in a time of great need for same.

Maya kept Penny and her baby safe. Baby Nina was three weeks premature and arrived with barely a warning sign. Unable to fetch the doc in time, Maya took charge and delivered a tiny but healthy specimen of a daughter. Equally as important she was able to coach Penny through the early nursing traumas with patience and compassion. It was as if she were a doctor, a doula, a medicine lady, and a mother, all wrapped up in one.

Penny once asked her if she had ever had children, ever been the mother she was serving her as? She had just smiled and shrugged, with that air of mystery that seemed always to surround her. Mother to Nina, mother to Penny, mother to the Free People. Maya was definitely a mother.

As the bad guys drifted away and Spring Town returned to some semblance of normalcy, Sammy and Penny increasingly longed to return to the lives they had known before the outside world had turned on them. The only scar tissue that remained was that on her arm where Jimmy Johnson's bullet had entered and exited, and poor Dr. Richard had tried to heal it. It all seemed so long ago and far away. Bad dream-like to her, but oh so very real.

Penny and Sammy kept their discussions to themselves for fear of sounding ungrateful to Maya and the others, but their restlessness was real.

"What would we do to earn an income?" Penny had asked Sammy one day. "After all, we have been living for free for almost two years, not a penny out of pocket."

Sammy knew that he could still fix things and that had once afforded him a comfortable single lifestyle before joining the university and later escaping to the woods in desperation. But now, there were three mouths to feed. No doubt their apartment had been turned over, and the car they had left in the parking space disposed of. So, they had no earthly goods except the clothes on their backs, which were all donated. And, they had each other.

They finally approached Maya in confidence and sought her opinion and, probably deep down, her blessing. They could never repay Maya for literally saving their lives and adding another to the mix.

Maya confirmed that they were obviously welcome to remain with the Free People and construct their own abode, with the help of others. She also understood their desire to return to the lives that had brought them together in the first place. She said that Lynda and Danny had come to her with similar musings and that she had encouraged them to follow their hearts. Penny sensed that she, too, was looking forward to getting back to a more solitary existence.

With the door to this discussion open, Penny and Sammy soon were trying to plan their exit to coincide with Lynda and Danny's. They had become very close after months of sharing a confining, if magical, lifestyle with Maya. They, too, were worried about re-entry and starting from scratch with nothing. They had all left behind bank accounts with small balances, which might be pooled together to afford a fresh start for all. They had lived together for almost two years and could surely continue to do so until able to afford the luxury of privacy.

The two couples finally worked up the courage to share their final plans with Maya. She smiled gently when they told her and left the room. They looked back and forth at each other, concerned that they had offended, or at least disappointed. Maya soon returned carrying two paper bags, handing one to each of us.

"A loan from the Free People Community Bank," she announced. "$20,000 cash for each of you to get started, interest-free of course, payable only when you have the means to do so, if ever. With our blessings and high hopes for your futures."

Penny started crying immediately and was soon joined by Lynda. This was beyond even the realm of kindness they had lived in these past few years. Danny and Sammy tried to be men, but even they both swallowed hard and teared up.

"Maya, you've saved our lives many times over, and now you help us start them over again."

"Penny and Sammy, you were the ones who took the big risks, who took on the man and his money, who stayed strong when others would have backed down or slipped off. You didn't murder a man, you killed a greedy bastard in self-defense. You didn't steal anything, you rescued a cache of incriminating evidence that ultimately brought down a corrupt and sinister international agribusiness conspiracy. Sure, we could have continued our

Posse raids and resistance messaging and lifestyle as Free People, but none of this would have come to an end without your courage and persistence. It is only appropriate for us to say 'thank you' to you all."

Two days later, they all hugged Maya goodbye, not knowing if they would ever see her again, then exited in Danny's car, carefully covering the entrance to her track from the dirt road leading out of the forest. Maya had slipped a small jade pendant into Penny's hand as she closed the car door. It felt strange yet dynamic to her. Penny looked deep into Maya's eyes and sensed love and strength. She promised herself to never forget that moment, even if she never saw her again.

Funny thing, thought Penny. They had all changed during their time in exile. Penny had gained weight and wrinkles. Sammy showed a slight hint of gray at his temples, probably stress-related. But not Maya. She looked and seemed exactly the same as when they first met. Timeless, Penny thought as she waved goodbye to her. And then she couldn't see her anymore, as if she had evaporated into the shadows. Penny would miss Maya.

With Maya's "loan" they were able to rent separate apartments in the same complex, buy a used car to share, and start looking for employment and income. Sammy had no problem getting back into the "fix-it" circuit. Danny and Lynda began to create, print, and sell cards for all occasions, featuring Lynda's sketches and Danny's limericks. They rented a small storefront and gradually moved from retail sales to a wholesale regional market to scale up their successful small business. Profits followed.

"As for me," Penny mused, "who would have guessed?"

Oh, yes. Dutch Tippler did win a Pulitzer Prize for his expose of the Coalition for Prosperity, as did the *Daily Half Dozen* for publishing "Posse Tracks."

Chapter Fifty-Three

MASTHEAD

THE SPRING TOWN GAZETTE
EXECUTIVE EDITOR, PENNY PLUM SPODE
OWNED AND PUBLISHED BY DOROTHY ROBBERNET
OMAHA, NEBRASKA

Penny's dream had come true. She had her own print newspaper to manage and edit. She alone was given responsibility for content, format, and editorial positioning. From beat reporter to executive editor, via the most circuitous route one could ever dream.

After the scheme was revealed, the Coalition had come crumbling down, and Dutch and the *Daily Half Dozen* had earned their accolades. Penny, Sammy, Danny, and Lynda were invited to Omaha to celebrate over a long weekend by Dorothy Robbernet, who covered all their expenses.

Dorothy pulled Penny aside at the first dinner party, which included many prestigious community leaders and spouses, as well as newspaper staff. She arranged to meet Penny, with Dutch, for breakfast the next morning.

"Penny, we all owe you a great debt of gratitude, *all*, including the world," she began as coffee was poured and eggs ordered. "But more specifically, Dutch and I. You have given our newspaper a breath of life in a dying industry and helped set us apart in the race to survive."

"You took the chance on our story, Dorothy, and Dutch did the heavy lifting. You owe me nothing," Penny responded, toying with the jade pendant around her neck.

"Not true, Penny. And I have a business proposition for you, if you are interested. The *Spring Town Gazette* has been shuttered ever since its editor was arrested by the FBI. The owner, a Mrs. Deacon Duncan, approached me after the 'Posse Tracks' runout to see if I had any interest in purchasing and reopening the paper. Under normal circumstances I would have said no immediately, but because of the central role the paper played in the unwinding of the Coalition, the history buff in me said, 'Let me think about it.'"

"Dorothy did more than think about it, Penny," said Dutch. "She came to me for corroboration of the whole convoluted glob of intertwined tentacles, from Mrs. Duncan's corrupt and 'disappeared' husband to deceased editor and Coalition heavyweight Benjamin Bottoms to beat reporter Penny Plum's discovery of a treasure trove of evidence in its bowels to Avarice Archibald's heavy-handed attempts to retrieve the documents, and the entire life and death saga that followed all the way to the publishing of 'Posse Tracks.'"

Penny had visibly cringed at the image of globs of intertwined tentacles, bringing a smile to Dutch's face.

"Penny, I don't think we can in good conscience let a place of such historical significance in the history of publishing go down, slip away, vanish into fragments of memories. In effect, the *Spring Town Gazette* has made our enterprise, directly and tangentially, what we are today, a survivor, a leader in independent journalism, an alternative universe to the big corporates. I want to acquire the *Gazette* and give you full responsibility for its future. You once mentioned to Dutch your love of the newspaper business and your hope to find a place in it someday. Well, we are offering you that opportunity today, to say thank you, and to honor our history."

Penny was speechless. She could only nod her yes.

—⚜—

The ensuing years were the best of Penny Plum Spode's medium-young life. She had her Sammy and her three children. She had her friends and visits from her 'back East' parents. She had her means to earn a living and give her a voice in encouraging her homeland to reclaim its heritage of entrepreneurship, small businesses, family farms ... and clean water. And she had fun.

Her version of the *Daily Half Dozen* played off the format of the mother ship but focused intensely on the Ozarks. Beyond the up-front national and international headlines and back page editorials, she added the usual stuff of weddings, births, and obits that hometown newspapers thrived on. Local crime was on the decline, which could be translated into a positive of sorts, and the resurgence of entrepreneurial activity from business to family farms to cleaning up the waters that had been so fouled by factory farming provided a consistent pool of optimism from which to pull. Community service journalism, as Penny called it, focused attention on areas of need in the community but went beyond to call for action and measure progress. Good things happened when the local paper took on a cause, promoted it with consistency, and measured progress toward resolution.

And then there was the Ozarks itself. The colorful history, the lore, the humor, the culture, the myths, the monsters, the stereotypes, the tall tales. There was not, nor would there ever be, any shortage of entertaining material, so Penny assigned one of the daily half dozen to just that, the Ozarks. Her readers loved it and shared with friends. Print media mind you, not digital. Circulation exploded, advertising revenues lagged, but subscription fees drove a profitable low overhead operation. Penny and her staff of one beat writer and one admin assistant produced the local copy, with the national stuff received digitally, and all printed and distributed locally. Everyone did anything that was needed to get out a daily, except for Monday, which was down time for all. It was a unique model, co-opting the best of modern technology with love of place, to make a difference in a community's life.

For her Ozarks column, she drew heavily on the masters: Vance Randolph, Donald Harrington, Brooks Blevins, Daniel Woodrell, Randi Philander, and the like. Her personal favorite was Randolph, who had ventured into the farthest corners of the Arkansas and Missouri Ozarks in search of material and produced academic-styled volumes that spoke to the unique culture he encountered and studied.

Almost like the Free People, to whom she owed so much and yet was reluctant to expose as a result of that debt. She could have written a month's worth of columns on Maya alone but would never break that bond of trust. She missed her greatly and often rubbed the jade pendant that hung around her neck, where once the keys to a safe deposit box full of explosive materials had rested. What a difference a decade makes.

But back to Randolph. Her favorite stories were not the racy ones he published in *Pissing in the Snow,* when the academics wouldn't include them with his other works. No, it was the "monsters" of the Ozarks that he interspersed among other tall tales. Executive Editor Penny really had fun with these.

When a farmer with a small passel of pigs that wandered within his fenced off back forty found several of them mutilated one morning, he reported the loss to the sheriff, who in turn issued a statement seeking information from others as to similar losses.

Once Penny stopped shivering at the memories of the Posse, the CAFOs, the pigs she executed in the name of resistance, the shot in the arm, and all that followed, a random Randolphian idea popped into her head. The lead on one of her daily half dozen the next morning read straight out of fiction presented as fact.

A GOWROW'S VICTIMS?

"Mutilated porkers may evidence a Gowrow (pronounced like 'cow') Intrusion?"

(continued on page 2)

Never in the history of the *Spring Town Gazette* had readers turned to page 2 with such alacrity. What greeted them there only fueled the frenzy.

"It was reported to the sheriff's office that a possible Gowrow sighting could explain the mutilation of pigs two nights ago. A source, who refused to be identified, said he saw a giant green lizard-like creature leaving his pasture after he had responded to multiple squeals in the middle of the night. He claimed that the creature was at least twenty feet long, brandished tusks and long claws, and featured horns along its spine. It did not respond to his spotlight but fled with several of his pigs dangling from its mouth."

"As far-fetched as this sounds, our research reveals that indeed there have been multiple reports of such activity over the years, dating back to the late 1800s and folklorist Vance Randolph's affirmation of a beast called a Gowrow, of approximately the same size and appearance as reported, of which he found evidence in a cave in Northwest Arkansas. The name Gowrow evokes from the eerie scream it emits when attacking principally livestock and other wild animals. It purportedly hatches from a soft-shelled egg as large as a beer keg. A search party has evidently been organized to scour caves in the region in pursuit of the creature.

"Trick or Treat, and Early Happy Halloween, the staff of the *Spring Town Gazette*"

Penny's readers loved it and clamored for more Ozarks Monster Tales. Dorothy Robbernet and Dutch Tippler guffawed from afar. Muted cries of "fake news" were lost amidst the gales of laughter. Even the national corporate press took note.

Penny obliged her audiences with feature after feature, from Snickelhoopus to Snawfus to Side-Hill Hoofers to Giasticutus, to Hoop Snakes who rolled after their targeted victims like a wheel before delivering a fatal bite. And so on.

Life was finally good. Again.

Oh, yes, *Hog Sty*, Penny's fictional chronicling of the Buffalo National River "win" back in the 2010s, was finally published and became a regional best seller.

Chapter Fifty-Four

HEREAFTER

Penny jerked upright from the big sycamore she had been leaning back on. Sound asleep.

It's like I had this long bad dream, she thought hazily to herself, albeit it with a happy ending.

It was so real, so graphic, so disturbing, so overwhelming, so inspiring.

And yet I am still sitting here where I dozed, staring at the hole of water where I learned to swim and fish and paddle a canoe here on Goose Creek. The same pool where my ancestors frolicked and splashed about nearly two centuries ago. Just down from where they built the log cabin that has since been preserved. Just below the mountain top where their remains are interred beneath mid-nineteenth-century gravestones.

I know how angry they would be to encounter the scum, the algae blooms, the murk, and the stench of their special sullied place. They would demand to know where all the darters, the crawdads, the bass, and perch are. They would insist on learning who allowed this desecration to happen.

Would they blame me?

I can't help it. I can't stop the tears from flowing.

Is this on me?

What? I feel a strong hand on my left shoulder.

"What's a pretty lady like you doing crying?"

I reach for the jade pendant around my neck for grounding.

THE END

FOOTNOTE: *Since the mid-1990s, when local controls on CAFOs in Iowa were eliminated by state legislators, there are 700 impaired waterways and 10,000 CAFOs to celebrate economic development.*

ABOUT THE AUTHOR

Todd Parnell is the retired President of Drury University, founding CEO of THE BANK in Springfield, Mo., civic leader, environmental advocate as co-founder of the Upper White River Basin Foundation and recently retired Chairman of the Missouri Clean Water Commission, and award-winning author inducted into the Missouri Writers Hall of Fame in 2012. He holds Masters degrees in Business Administration from Dartmouth University and History from Missouri State University, and an undergraduate degree from Drury University.

Parnell began writing non-fiction during his years as a banker and educator, including published works *The Buffalo, Ben, and Me, Trails of the Heart: Along the Buffalo River, Mom at War,* and *Postcards from Branson.* He tried his hand at fiction upon retiring from the Drury presidency and hasn't stopped writing since, publishing the Ozarkian Folk Tales Trilogy (*Skunk Creek, Swine Branch,* and *Donny Brook*), with a second trilogy, Children of the Creek in production. Recently released are *Pig Farm*, the sweeping and rollicking historical tall tale set in the context of a real time environmental tragedy, and *Privilege and Privation-A Love Story* (2019), a tale of two young people from diverse economic backgrounds who fall in love and how the disparity affects their relationship and that of the people in their lives.

Parnell was born in Branson, Mo. and is an eighth-generation Ozarker. He resides with his wife of 42 years, Betty, in Springfield, Mo. and is blessed with four children and five grandchildren. The Parnells were inaugural co-chairs of the Every Child Promise initiative, and serve on its executive advisory board.

ALSO BY TODD PARNELL

Pig Farm is a taste of the present spread over two centuries past, eight generations of the fictional Snarkle clan in all, grounded in the truth of a non-fictional travesty. It's an historical tall tale set in the context of a real-life environmental tragedy.

Brimming with humor and colorful characters, riddled with mystery and misfortune, tainted with prejudice and deceit, and laced with money and greed, fiction intersects with fact to paint a disturbing portrait of a "pig farm" over time.

At its core, Pig Farm is a recounting of how an ill-conceived and stupidly-permitted pig CAFO alongside the Buffalo National River might have come to be.

Privilege and Privation—A Love Story is a tale of two young people from immensely different backgrounds who fall in love, set amidst the contradictions of "haves" and "have nots," the violence and hopelessness of the deprived, and the dreams and hypocrisy of the privileged.

The story line follows the fortunes of Lenny, a middle class kid, and Lucy, a child born in poverty, from their earliest years. It highlights the impact of parental involvement, quality early childhood care and education, and recognition of each's special gifts on the developmental process. It is a tragedy, a love story, and most importantly, a vision of hope.

www.ingramcontent.com/pod-product-compliance
Lightning Source LLC
Chambersburg PA
CBHW031656030726
47494CB00007BB/2103